Maigret Gets Angry

'I love reading Simenon. He makes me think of Chekhov'
— William Faulkner

'A truly wonderful writer . . . marvellously readable – lucid, simple, absolutely in tune with the world he creates'
— Muriel Spark

'Few writers have ever conveyed with such a sure touch, the bleakness of human life'
— A. N. Wilson

'One of the greatest writers of the twentieth century . . . Simenon was unequalled at making us look inside, though the ability was masked by his brilliance at absorbing us obsessively in his stories'
— *Guardian*

'A novelist who entered his fictional world as if he were part of it'
— Peter Ackroyd

'The greatest of all, the most genuine novelist we have had in literature'
— André Gide

'Superb . . . The most addictive of writers . . . A unique teller of tales'
— *Observer*

'The mysteries of the human personality are revealed in all their disconcerting complexity'
— Anita Brookner

'A writer who, more than any other crime novelist, combined a high literary reputation with popular appeal'
— P. D. James

'A supreme writer . . . Unforgettable vividness' – *Independent*

'Compelling, remorseless, brilliant'
— John Gray

'Extraordinary masterpieces of the twentieth century'
— John Banville

GEORGES SIMENON

Maigret Gets Angry

Translated by ROS SCHWARTZ

PENGUIN BOOKS

PENGUIN CLASSICS

UK | USA | Canada | Ireland | Australia
India | New Zealand | South Africa

Penguin Books is part of the Penguin Random House group of companies
whose addresses can be found at global.penguinrandomhouse.com.

Penguin
Random House
UK

First published in French as *Maigret se fâche* by Presses de la Cité 1947
This translation first published 2015

010

Set in Dante MT Std 12.5/15 pt
Typeset by Palimpsest Book Production Limited, Falkirk, Stirlingshire
Printed and bound in Great Britain by Clays Ltd, Elcograf S.p.A.

ISBN: 978-0-141-39732-0

Contents

Contents

1. *The Old Lady in the Garden*

Madame Maigret sat shelling peas in the warm shade, the blue of her apron and the green of the pea pods making rich splashes of colour. Her hands were never still, even though it was two o'clock in the afternoon on the hottest day of a sweltering August. She was keeping an eye on her husband as if he were a babe-in-arms. Madame Maigret was anxious:

'I bet you're already getting up.'

And yet the deck chair in which Maigret lay hadn't creaked, nor had the former detective chief inspector of the Police Judiciaire let out the faintest sigh.

Probably because she knew him so well, she had seen his face shiny with sweat quiver imperceptibly. She was right, he was about to get up. But he forced himself to remain horizontal out of a sort of human respect.

This was the second summer they were spending in their house in Meung-sur-Loire since he had retired. Maigret had ensconced himself contentedly in the comfortable canvas chair, puffing away gently at his pipe. He savoured the coolness of the air around him all the more since only two metres away, on the other side of the boundary between shade and sunshine, it was an inferno buzzing with flies.

The peas tumbled into the enamel basin at a regular

rhythm. Sitting with her knees apart, Madame Maigret had an apronful, and there were two big basketfuls picked that morning for bottling.

What Maigret loved most about his house was this spot where they were sitting, a place that had no name, a sort of partially roofed courtyard between the kitchen and the garden which they had gradually furnished, even putting in an oven and a dresser, and where they ate most of their meals. Slightly reminiscent of a Spanish patio, it was paved with red floor tiles that gave the shadows a very special character.

Maigret held out for a good five minutes, maybe a little longer, gazing through his half-closed eyelids at the vegetable garden that seemed to be steaming under a blistering sun. Then, setting aside all human respect, he got up.

'Now what are you going to do?'

Off-guard in this domestic intimacy, his expression was that of a sulking child caught misbehaving.

'I'm sure the aubergines are covered in Colorado beetles again,' he grumbled, 'and that's because of *your* lettuces . . .'

This little battle over the lettuces had been going on for a month. Since Madame Maigret had put her lettuce seedlings in the gaps between the aubergine plants.

'It's a pity to waste the space,' she had said.

At that point, he had not protested, because he hadn't realized that Colorado beetles love aubergine leaves even more than potatoes. But he couldn't spray them with an arsenic mixture because of the lettuces.

And ten times a day, Maigret, wearing his huge straw

hat, would go and bend over the pale-green leaves, as he was doing now, turning them over gently to pick off the little striped insects. He kept them in his left hand until it was full, and then he tossed them into the bonfire, looking disgruntled and darting a defiant glance at his wife.

'If you hadn't planted those lettuces . . .'

The fact was that since he had retired she hadn't seen him sit still for an hour in his famous deck chair, which he had triumphantly brought back from the Bazar de l'Hôtel-de-Ville swearing that he would have memorable siestas in it.

There he was, in the heat of the sun, barefoot in his wooden clogs, his blue linen trousers riding down his hips, making them look like an elephant's hindquarters, and a farmer's shirt with an intricate pattern that was open at the neck, revealing his hairy chest.

He heard the sound of the door knocker echoing through the dark, empty rooms of the house like a bell in a convent. Someone was at the front door, and, as always when there was an unexpected visitor, Madame Maigret became flustered. She looked at him from a distance as if to seek his guidance.

She lifted up her apron, which formed a huge pouch, wondered what to do with her peas, then finally untied the strings, because she would never go and open the door looking unkempt.

The knocker clanged again, twice, three times, imperiously, angrily, from the sound of it. Maigret thought he could make out the gentle purr of a car engine through the quivering of the air. He continued to tend his aubergines while his wife tidied her grey hair in front of a fragment of mirror.

She had barely disappeared inside the dark house when the little green door in the garden wall that led on to the lane, and was used only by people they knew, opened. An elderly lady in mourning appeared in the doorway, so stiff, so severe, and at the same time so comical that he would recall the sight of her for a long time.

She stood there for only a moment, and then, with a brisk, decisive step that belied her great age, she marched straight towards Maigret.

'I say, gardener . . . There's no point telling me that your master's not at home . . . I know for a fact that he is here.'

She was tall and thin, with a crinkled face caked in a thick layer of powder streaked with sweat. The most striking thing about her was her extraordinarily lively eyes of an intense black.

'Go at once and tell him that Bernadette Amorelle has come a hundred kilometres to talk to him.'

She certainly hadn't had the patience to linger at the front door. She would not be kept waiting! As she said, she had asked the neighbours and had not been deterred by the closed shutters.

Had someone told her about the little garden door? It wouldn't have mattered, she was capable of finding it for herself. And now she was walking towards the shady courtyard where Madame Maigret had just reappeared.

'Kindly tell Detective Chief Inspector Maigret . . .'

Madame Maigret was baffled. Her husband followed

with a lumbering tread, an amused twinkle in his eye. It was he who said:

'If you would like to trouble yourself to come in.'

'He's having a nap, I'll wager. Is he still as fat?'

'Do you know him well?'

'What business is it of yours? Go and tell him that Bernadette Amorelle is here and never mind anything else.'

She had second thoughts, rummaged in her bag, an outmoded kind, a black velvet reticule with a silver clasp, the sort that was fashionable around 1900.

'Here,' she said, proffering a small banknote.

'Forgive me for not being able to accept, Madame Amorelle, but I am former Detective Chief Inspector Maigret.'

Then she said something hilarious, which was to go down in the annals of the Maigret household. Looking him up and down from his clogs to his dishevelled hair – for he had removed his huge straw hat – she proclaimed:

'As you wish . . .'

Poor Madame Maigret! She gesticulated to her husband, but he didn't notice. She was trying to signal discreetly to him to take the visitor into the sitting room. One doesn't entertain in a courtyard that serves as a kitchen and everything else.

But Madame Amorelle had sat herself down in a little rattan armchair where she was perfectly comfortable. It was she who, noticing Madame Maigret's nervousness, said to her impatiently:

'Let the inspector be!'

She all but asked Madame Maigret to leave them,

which is exactly what the latter did, because she didn't dare continue with her task in the presence of the visitor, and she didn't know where to put herself.

'You recognize my name, don't you, inspector?'

'Amorelle, of the sand quarries and tug-boats?'

'Amorelle and Campois, yes.'

He had carried out an investigation in the Haute Seine in the past, and all day long he had watched convoys of boats going past bearing the green Amorelle and Campois triangle. When he was based at Quai des Orfèvres, he often used to glimpse the offices of Amorelle and Campois, quarry and ship owners, on the Île St Louis.

'I have no time to waste and you must understand me. Earlier, I took advantage of the fact that my son-in-law and daughter were at the Maliks' to tell François to get the old Renault going . . . They don't suspect anything . . . They probably won't be home before this evening . . . Do you understand?'

'No . . . Yes . . .'

What he did understand was that the elderly lady had sneaked out, unbeknown to her family.

'I assure you that if they were to find out I was here—'

'Excuse me, where were you?'

'At Orsenne, of course,' she answered, the way a queen of France might have said: 'At Versailles!'

Didn't everyone know, shouldn't everyone know, that Bernadette Amorelle, of Amorelle and Campois, lived at Orsenne, a little hamlet on the banks of the Seine between Corbeil and the forest of Fontainebleau?

'There's no point looking at me as if you think I'm mad.

They'll probably try and have you believe I am. I assure you it's not true.'

'Forgive me, madame, but may I ask your age?'

'You may, young man. I'll be eighty-two on the seventh of September . . . but my teeth are all my own, if that's what you're looking at . . . And I'll probably outlive the lot of them . . . I'd be very happy to see my son-in-law go to his grave.'

'Would you like something to drink?'

'A glass of cold water, if you have some.'

He poured it himself.

'What time did you leave Orsenne?'

'At eleven thirty . . . As soon as they'd gone . . . I had already asked François . . . François is the gardener's boy, he's a good boy . . . I helped his mother bring him into the world . . . None of the family knows that he can drive an automobile . . . One night when I couldn't sleep – I should tell you, inspector, that I never sleep – I found him trying his hand at driving the old Renault by moonlight. Does this interest you?'

'It does indeed.'

'It doesn't take much . . . The old Renault, which wasn't even in the garage but in the stables, is a limousine that belonged to my late husband . . . Since he died twenty years ago, it must be . . . Well, the boy somehow managed to get it going and would take it for a spin on the road at night.'

'Did he drive you here?'

'He's waiting for me outside.'

'You haven't had lunch?'

'I eat when I have time . . . I hate people who constantly feel the need to eat.'

And she couldn't help darting a disapproving look at Maigret's paunch.

'Look how you're sweating. It's none of my business . . . My husband, he also insisted on having his own way and he's been gone for a long time . . . You've been retired for two years now, isn't that so?'

'Nearly two years, yes.'

'So you're getting bored . . . You will agree to my proposal, then. There's a train at five o'clock from Orléans. I could drop you off at the station on my way back. Of course, it would be easier to drive you all the way to Orsenne, but you would not go unnoticed and the whole thing would go wrong.'

'Forgive me, madame, but—'

'I know you're going to protest. But I absolutely need you to come and spend a few days at Orsenne. Fifty thousand if you're successful. And, if you find nothing, let's say ten thousand plus your expenses.'

She opened her bag and took out a wad of notes.

'There's an inn. There's no chance of mistaking it as it's the only one. It's called L'Ange. You'll be extremely uncomfortable there, since poor Jeanne is half-crazy. Another one I knew as a baby. She might not want to put you up, but you'll find a way of winning her over, I'm sure. Just start talking to her about ailments, and she'll be happy. She's convinced she's got them all.'

Madame Maigret brought in a tray with some coffee, and the elderly lady, indifferent to this gesture, rebuffed her:

'What's this? Who told you to bring us coffee? Take it away!'

She took her for the maid, as she had mistaken Maigret for the gardener.

'I could tell you lots of stories, but I know your reputation and I know that you are clever enough to find things out for yourself. Don't be taken in by my son-in-law, that's my only piece of advice. He has hoodwinked everyone. He is polite, more so than anyone you've ever met. He's sickeningly polite. But one day his head will roll—'

'I'm sorry, madame—'

'Stop saying sorry, inspector. I had a granddaughter, just one, the daughter of this wretched Malik. My son-in-law is called Malik, that too you should know. Charles Malik . . . My granddaughter, Monita, would have turned eighteen next week—'

'You mean she's dead?'

'Exactly seven days ago. We buried her the day before yesterday. She was found drowned, on the weir downstream . . . And, when Bernadette Amorelle tells you that it was no accident, you can believe it. Monita could swim like a fish. People will try and have you believe that she was reckless, that she used to go swimming alone at six o'clock in the morning and sometimes at night. That wouldn't have caused her to drown. And if they insinuate that perhaps she wanted to commit suicide, you can tell them that they're lying.'

The conversation had switched abruptly from comedy to tragedy, but the curious thing was that the old lady's tone remained that of comedy. She did not cry. There wasn't the hint of a tear in her startlingly black eyes. Her entire sharp, twitchy being continued to be animated with the same vitality, which, in spite of everything, had something comical about it.

She forged on, pursuing her train of thought with no regard for customary niceties. She looked at Maigret without doubting for a moment that he was all hers, simply because that was what she wanted.

She had stolen away in secret, in a dubious automobile, with a kid who could barely drive, crossing the entire Beauce region in the heat of the day, forgoing lunch. Now, she was looking at the time on an old-fashioned necklace watch that she was wearing.

'If you have any questions, be quick,' she commanded, already poised to get up.

'You don't like your son-in-law, if I understand correctly.'

'I hate him.'

'Does your daughter hate him too? Is she unhappy with him?'

'I don't know and I don't care.'

'Don't you get on with your daughter?'

'I prefer to ignore her. She has no spine, no blood in her veins.'

'You say that seven days ago, in other words last Tuesday, your granddaughter drowned in the Seine.'

'I most certainly did not. You'd better listen more carefully to what I tell you. Monita was found dead in the Seine, on the weir downstream.'

'But she had no injuries and the doctor gave permission for the body to be buried?'

She merely looked at him with the utmost contempt, with perhaps a touch of pity.

'You are the only person, I gather, who suspects that this death was not natural.'

This time, she rose.

'Listen, inspector. You are reputed to be the cleverest policeman in the whole of France. At least the one who has had the most successes. Get dressed. Pack your bag. In half an hour I'm dropping you off at Les Aubrais station. By seven o'clock this evening, you'll be at the Auberge de l'Ange. It would be best if we appeared not to know one another. Every day, at around midday, François will go and have a drink at L'Ange. He doesn't usually drink, but I'll order him to. So that we can communicate without arousing their suspicions.'

She took a few steps in the direction of the garden, determined no doubt to go for a stroll while waiting for him, despite the heat.

'Hurry up.'

Then, turning around:

'Perhaps you would be so kind as to have a drink brought out to François. He must be in the car. Wine mixed with water. Not pure wine, as he has to drive me home, and he's not used to it.'

Madame Maigret, who must have overheard everything, was standing in the hall behind the door.

'What are you doing, Maigret?' she asked on seeing him head for the staircase with its copper banister knob.

It was cool inside the house, where there was a pleasant smell of wax polish, cut hay, ripening fruit and food simmering on the stove. It had taken Maigret fifty years to rediscover that smell, the smell of his childhood, of his parents' house.

'You're not going to go with that mad old woman, are you?'

He had left his clogs by the door. He walked barefoot on the cool tiles, then up the polished oak stairs.

'Give the driver a drink, then come upstairs and help me pack.'

There was a little twinkle in his eyes, a little twinkle he recognized as he shaved in cold water and looked at himself in the bathroom mirror.

'I really don't understand you,' sighed his wife. 'Only a couple of hours ago you couldn't relax because of a few Colorado beetles.'

The train. He was hot. He sat in his corner puffing on his pipe. The grass on the embankments was yellow, the little stations with their tubs of flowers flashed past. In the haze of the heat a man waved his small red flag and blew a whistle, as children do, looking ridiculous.

Maigret was greying at the temples. He was a little calmer, a little heavier than he had been, but he did not feel that he had aged since retiring from the Police Judiciaire.

It was out of vanity, or rather a sort of modesty, that for the past two years he had systematically refused to take on any of the jobs he had been offered, especially by banks, insurance companies and jewellers, who brought him tricky cases.

At Quai des Orfèvres they would have said:

'Poor old Maigret's going back to his old ways, he's already bored with gardening and fishing.'

And here he was, having allowed an old woman who had appeared through the little green door to twist him round her little finger.

He pictured her sitting upright and dignified in the old-fashioned limousine driven with perilous negligence by a François still wearing his gardener's clothes who hadn't had time to swap his clogs for a pair of shoes.

He heard her saying, after she had seen Madame Maigret waving from the doorstep as they left:

'That's your wife, isn't it? She must have been offended when I took her for the housekeeper . . . And I thought you were the gardener.'

And the car set off on its daredevil journey, having dropped Maigret off at Les Aubrais station in Orléans, where François, in the wrong gear, had nearly reversed into a whole cluster of bicycles.

It was the holiday season. Parisians swarmed all over the countryside and the woods, driving fast cars on the roads and paddling canoes on the rivers, and there were fishermen in straw boaters at the foot of every willow tree.

Orsenne wasn't a station, but a halt where the occasional train condescended to stop. Through the trees in the vast gardens the roofs of large houses could be glimpsed, and beyond them the Seine, broad and majestic at this spot.

Maigret would have found it hard to say why he had obeyed Bernadette Amorelle's orders. Perhaps because of the Colorado beetles?

Suddenly, he too felt as if he were on holiday, just like the people he had sat among on the train, those he met walking down the steep path, those he saw everywhere since he had left Meung.

A different atmosphere from that of his garden enveloped him. He walked with a light step amid his new surroundings. At the bottom of the sloping path, he came to the Seine bordered by a track wide enough for vehicle traffic.

From the station, Maigret had followed the signs with arrows indicating the Auberge de l'Ange. He entered a garden with neglected arbours, and finally pushed open the glass door of a veranda where the air was suffocating because of the sunshine streaming in through the glazed sides.

'Hello!' he called.

There was only a cat on a cushion on the floor and some fishing rods in a corner.

'Hello!'

He descended a step and found himself in a room where the copper pendulum of an ancient clock swung lazily to and fro, clicking with each movement.

'There's no one in this dump,' he muttered.

Just then someone stirred, close to where he stood. He shuddered and in the gloom could just make out a person moving. It was a woman wrapped in blankets, no doubt this Jeanne whom Madame Amorelle had mentioned. Her dark, greasy hair hung down on either side of her face and there was a thick white compress around her neck.

'We're closed!' she croaked.

'I know, madame. I heard you were unwell.'

Ouch! The word 'unwell', ridiculously inadequate, was an insult.

'I'm at death's door, you mean! Nobody will believe it . . . People are horrible.'

Nevertheless, she finished shrugging off the blanket covering her legs and got to her feet, her thick ankles swollen over the tops of her felt slippers.

'Who sent you here?'

'It so happens I came here once before, more than twenty years ago, and this is a sort of pilgrimage that—'

'So you knew Marius?'

'Of course I did!'

'Poor Marius . . . You know he died?'

'So I heard. I found it hard to believe.'

'Why? . . . He wasn't in good health either . . . It's three years since he died, and here I am, dragging on . . . Were you expecting to sleep here?'

She had spotted the suitcase that he had left in the doorway.

'I was planning to spend a few days here, yes. As long as I'm not putting you to any trouble. In your condition—'

'Have you come far?'

'From the Orléans area.'

'You don't have a car?'

'No. I came by train.'

'And there are no trains back today. Oh Lord! Oh Lord! Raymonde! Raymonde! . . . I bet she's off gallivanting again. I'm going to have to have words with her . . . If she'll listen . . . Because she can be difficult. She's the maid, but she takes advantage of my being unwell to do as she pleases and anyone would think she was the one in charge. Well, well, now what does *he* want around here?'

She was looking out of the window at a man whose footsteps could be heard crunching the gravel. Maigret watched him too and began to frown, for the newcomer vaguely reminded him of someone.

He was wearing tennis whites or country attire, white flannel trousers, a white jacket and shoes, but what struck Maigret was his black crepe armband.

He came in, as if he were a regular.

'Hello, Jeanne.'

'What do you want, Monsieur Malik?'

'I came to ask if you—'

He stopped mid-sentence, looked straight at Maigret and broke into a smile, saying:

'Jules! . . . Well I never! . . . What on earth are *you* doing here?'

'I'm sorry?'

First of all, it had been years and years since anyone had called him Jules, to the extent that he had almost forgotten his first name. Even his wife was in the habit of calling him Maigret, which he found amusing.

'Don't you remember?'

'No . . .'

Yet that ruddy face with well-defined features, a prominent nose, cold, steely eyes, was no stranger to him. The name Malik too, when Madame Amorelle had uttered it, had rung a bell somewhere in the back of his mind.

'Ernest.'

'Ernest who?'

Hadn't Bernadette Amorelle spoken of a Charles Malik?

'The Moulins lycée.'

Maigret had been a pupil at the lycée in Moulins for three years when his father was the estate manager at a chateau in the region. Still . . .

Curiously, although his memory was unreliable, he was certain that it was an unpleasant recollection that this well-groomed face, this man brimming with self-confidence, stirred in him. What was more, he did not like his over-friendly manner. He had always had a horror of familiarity.

'The Tax Collector.'

'I'm with you, yes . . . I would never have recognized you.'

'What are you doing here?'

'Me? I—'

Malik burst out laughing.

'We'll talk about it later . . . I knew perfectly well that Detective Chief Inspector Maigret was none other than my old pal Jules. Do you remember the English teacher? . . . No need to make up a room, Jeanne. My friend will stay at the house.'

'No!' protested Maigret, annoyed.

'Eh? What did you say?'

'I said that I'd stay here . . . It's already been arranged with Jeanne.'

'Are you sure?'

'I insist.'

'Because of the old woman?'

'What old woman?'

A mischievous smile hovered on Ernest Malik's thin lips, the smile of the schoolboy he had once been.

He was nicknamed the Tax Collector because his father was the tax collector in Moulins. He was very thin, with a hatchet face and light-coloured eyes, of an unappealing grey.

'Don't worry, Jules. You'll understand later . . . Tell us, Jeanne, don't be afraid to speak your mind. Is my mother-in-law mad, yes or no?'

And Jeanne, gliding noiselessly in her slippers, muttered half-heartedly:

'I'd rather not get involved in your family affairs.'

She was already viewing Maigret less sympathetically, if not with distrust.

'Well, are you staying here or are you going with him?'

'I'm staying.'

Malik was still looking at his former schoolmate mockingly, as if this were all a prank being played on Maigret.

'You're going to have a lot of fun, I assure you . . . I can't think of anywhere more lively than the Auberge de l'Ange. You saw the angel, you were taken in!'

Did he suddenly recall that he was in mourning? In any case, his manner became more solemn as he added:

'If all this weren't so sad, we'd have a good laugh, the two of us . . . Come up to the house at least. Yes, you must! You have to . . . I'll explain . . . I'll tell you over an aperitif and you'll get the picture.'

Maigret was still in two minds. He stood rooted to the spot, massive compared to his companion, who was the same height as him but unusually slim.

'I'll come,' he eventually said, somewhat reluctantly.

'You'll dine with us, of course? I can't pretend the house is very cheerful at the moment, after the death of my niece, but . . .'

As they left, Maigret glimpsed Jeanne, who sat watching them from a dark corner. And he had the impression that there was hatred in the look that she allowed to rest on Ernest Malik's elegant form.

2. *The Tax Collector's Second Son*

As the two men walked along the riverbank, they must have given the impression that one had the other on a leash, as if the latter, surly and clumsy, was letting himself be dragged along like a big, shaggy dog.

And the truth is that Maigret was ill-at-ease. Already, in their schooldays, he had had no fondness for the Tax Collector. What was more, he abhorred those people from the past who suddenly pop up and give you a friendly tap on the shoulder and treat you with familiarity.

In short, Ernest Malik was the type who had always made his hackles rise.

Meanwhile Malik walked nonchalantly, relaxed in his immaculately cut white-flannel suit, his person well groomed, his hair lustrous and his skin dry despite the heat. He was already playing the lord of the manor showing a country bumpkin around his estate.

There was a sardonic glint in his eyes, as there always had been, even when he was a boy, a furtive glint that said: 'I've got you and I'll get you again . . . I'm so much smarter than you!'

The Seine, on their left, meandered lazily and was very wide at this point, fringed with reeds. On their right, low walls, some of them very ancient, others almost new, separated the towpath from the houses.

They were few: four or five, as far as Maigret could tell. They looked opulent, set in extensive, well-maintained grounds, the paths visible through the metal railings.

'This house belongs to my mother-in-law, whom you had the pleasure of meeting today,' announced Malik as they reached a big gate with pilasters surmounted by stone lions. 'Old Amorelle bought it, some forty years ago, from a Second Empire finance magnate.'

A vast edifice appeared, surrounded by trees. It was not particularly attractive, but solid and affluent. Tiny revolving sprinklers were watering the lawns, while an elderly gardener who looked as if he was out of a seed merchant's catalogue was raking the paths.

'What do you think of Bernadette Amorelle?' asked Malik, turning to his former schoolmate and looking him straight in the eye, his gaze twinkling with mischief.

Maigret mopped his forehead. Malik seemed to be saying: 'Poor old thing, you haven't changed. You're still the clumsy son of an estate manager! A big country oaf. Full of naivety and perhaps some common sense!'

And out loud:

'Keep going . . . I live a little further on, after the bend. Do you remember my brother? . . . True, you didn't know him at school, because he's three years younger than us. My brother Charles married one of the Amorelle girls a couple of years after I married the eldest . . . He lives in this house in the summer with his wife and our mother-in-law. It's his daughter who died last week.'

A hundred metres further on, they passed a gleaming

white pontoon, as luxurious as those of the prestigious yacht clubs on the banks of the Seine.

'This is the beginning of my estate . . . I have a few small boats, because a man has to have some fun in this godforsaken hole . . . Do you sail?'

What irony in his voice as he asked the burly Maigret if he sailed in one of those frail barques that could be seen between the mooring buoys!

'This way . . .'

Railings topped with gilt arrows. A glistening white-sand drive. The gardens sloped gently and soon a modern building came into view, much bigger than the Amorelles' house. Tennis courts to the left, dark red in the sunshine. A swimming pool to the right.

And Malik, increasingly offhand, like a pretty woman playing carelessly with a jewel worth millions, seemed to be saying: 'Look closely, you great oaf, this is the Maliks' place. Yes, young Malik scornfully nicknamed the Tax Collector because his daddy spent his days behind a grille in a dreary office.'

Two huge Great Danes came and licked his hands and he accepted this meek homage, appearing not to notice.

'We can have an aperitif on the terrace if you like while we wait for the dinner gong . . . My son must be boating on the Seine . . .'

Behind the house, a driver in shirt-sleeves was hosing a powerful American car with gleaming chrome trims.

They climbed the steps and settled themselves in wide rattan armchairs, like club chairs, under a red sunshade. A butler in a white jacket hurried over, reinforcing Maigret's feeling that he was at a luxury hotel in a spa town rather than a private residence.

'Rosé? . . . Martini? . . . Manhattan? . . . What's your favourite tipple, Jules? If what the papers say about you is true, you like a beer at the bar? . . . Sorry to say I haven't put a bar in here yet . . . One day, maybe . . . That would be quite fun. Two Martinis, Jean! You're very welcome to smoke your pipe. Where were we? Oh yes! . . . My brother and my sister-in-law are of course pretty devastated by this business . . . They only had the one daughter, you see. My sister-in-law has never enjoyed good health . . .'

Was Maigret listening? If he was, he wasn't aware of it. And yet, Malik's words automatically etched themselves in his memory.

Ensconced in his chair, his eyes half-closed, a warm pipe between his sullen lips, he gazed vaguely at the scenery, which was very beautiful. The setting sun was turning red. From the terrace where they were sitting, they could see the entire loop of the Seine, the opposite bank edged by wooded hillsides where a quarry made a crude white gash.

A few white sails were moving over the dark, silken water, a few varnished canoes glided slowly, a motor-boat buzzed, and after it had vanished into the distance, the noise of its engine still hung in the air.

The butler had set down in front of them crystal glasses which misted over.

'This morning, I invited both of them to spend the day here at the house. No point inviting my mother-in-law. She's a woman who loathes family and who has been known to stay shut up in her room for weeks on end.'

His smile proclaimed: 'You can't understand, poor, over-weight Maigret. You're used to little people who lead ordinary little lives and who can't permit themselves the slightest eccentricity.'

And it was true that Maigret did not feel at home in this milieu. The decor itself irritated him – it was too harmonious, its lines too smooth. He even came to hate the neat tennis court and the overfed driver he had seen polishing the sumptuous car – and it wasn't envy because he wasn't *that* small-minded. The pontoon, with its diving boards, the little boats moored around it, the swimming pool, the pruned trees and the immaculate white-sand paths all belonged to a world he was reluctant to enter and which made him feel awkward and heavy.

'I'm telling you all this to explain why I turned up at the good Jeanne's earlier. When I say "the good Jeanne", it's a manner of speaking, because she's actually the most deceitful creature on this earth. When her husband was alive, her Marius, she used to be unfaithful to him all the time. Now that he's dead, she laments him from dawn to dusk.

'So my brother and my sister-in-law were here. When we were about to sit down to lunch, my sister-in-law realizes that she's forgotten her pills. She's on medication. Her nerves, she says. I offer to go and fetch them. Instead of going via the road, I go through the gardens since our properties are adjacent.

'I happen to look down. As I walk past the old stables, I notice tyre tracks. I open the door and I'm flabbergasted to see that my late father-in-law's old limousine has gone . . .

'That, my friend, is how I ended up meeting you. I talked to the gardener, who admitted that his boy had gone off an hour earlier with the car and that Bernadette had been with him.

'When they got home, I called the boy to me and questioned him. I found out that he had gone to Meung-sur-Loire and that he had dropped a fat man with a suitcase at Les Aubrais station. Apologies, old friend. His words, not mine.

'I immediately thought that my charming mother-in-law had gone to talk to some private detective, because she has persecution mania and she's convinced that there's something sinister behind her granddaughter's death.

'I confess I didn't think of you . . . I knew that there was a Maigret in the police, but I wasn't sure that it was the Jules I was at school with.

'What do you have to say about that?'

And Maigret replied:

'Nothing.'

He said nothing. He was thinking about his house that was so different, about his garden with its aubergines, about the peas dropping into the enamel basin, and he wondered why he had meekly followed the dictatorial old lady who had literally kidnapped him.

He was thinking about the train, humming with heat, his former office at Quai des Orfèvres, about all the scum he had interrogated, about the many little bars, insalubrious hotels, improbable places where his investigations had taken him.

He was thinking about all that and he was all the more

furious, more annoyed at being there, in a hostile environment, under the Tax Collector's sardonic gaze.

'Later, if you like, I'll give you a guided tour of the house. I drew the plans myself with the architect. Of course, we don't live here all year round, only in summer. I have an apartment in Paris, Avenue Hoche. I've also bought a house three kilometres outside Deauville, and we went there in July. In August, with all the crowds, the seaside is impossible. Now, if you fancy it, I'd be delighted to invite you to spend a few days with us. Do you play tennis? Do you ride?'

Why didn't he ask him if he played golf too and whether he water-skied?

'Mind you, if you attach the slightest importance to what my mother-in-law told you, I wouldn't dream of getting in the way of your little investigation. I place myself at your service and if you need a car and a driver . . . Ah! Here's my wife.'

She emerged from the house, also dressed in white.

'Let me introduce Maigret, an old school friend . . . My wife . . .'

She extended a pale, limp hand at the end of a pale arm. Everything about her was pale – her face and her hair that was a too-light blonde.

'Do please sit down, monsieur.'

What was it about her that exuded a sense of unease? Perhaps the fact that she seemed somehow absent? Her voice was neutral, so impersonal that one wondered whether it was she who had spoken. She sat down in a big armchair, giving the impression that she might just as well have been somewhere else. And yet she gave her husband a discreet signal, which he didn't understand. She raised her eyes towards the single upper floor, and said:

'It's Georges-Henry.'

Then, frowning, Malik rose, saying to Maigret:

'Would you excuse me for a minute?'

They sat there, still and silent, the wife and the inspector, and then suddenly, from upstairs, a rumpus broke out. A door was flung open. Rapid footsteps. One of the windows banged shut. Muffled voices. The echoes of an argument, most likely, or in any case, a fairly heated exchange.

All that Madame Malik could find to say was:

'You've never been to Orsenne before?'

'No, madame.'

'It's quite pretty if you like the countryside. It's very restful, isn't it?'

And the way she pronounced the word 'restful' gave it a very particular emphasis. She was so listless, so weary perhaps, or had such little life in her, her body abandoned itself with such inertia in the rattan chair that she was the picture of restfulness, eternal rest.

And yet she was listening out for the noises upstairs, which were subsiding and, when all was quiet, she said:

'I understand you're having dinner with us?'

Well-brought-up as she was, she was unable to appear pleased, even out of mere politeness. It was a statement. There was a note of regret in her voice. Malik came back, and, when Maigret looked at him, he once again put on his pinched smile.

27

'Will you excuse me? . . . . There's always trouble with the servants.'

They waited for the dinner gong with a certain awkwardness. In his wife's presence, Malik seemed less relaxed.

'Jean-Claude isn't back yet?'

'I think I can see him on the pontoon.'

A young man in shorts had just stepped off a light sailing boat which he tied up before walking slowly towards the house, his sweater over his arm. Just then, the gong sounded, and they moved into the dining room, where they would soon be joined by Ernest Malik's eldest son Jean-Claude, washed, combed and dressed in grey flannel.

'If I had known sooner that you were coming I would have invited my brother and my sister-in-law, so that you could meet the entire family. I'll ask them tomorrow, if you like, as well as our neighbours – we don't have many. Our place is where we all get together . . . There are nearly always guests . . . People come and go, they make themselves at home.'

The dining room was vast and sumptuous. The table was of pink-veined marble and the cutlery was placed on little individual table mats.

'In short, from what the papers have said about you, you had quite a successful career in the police? Strange profession. I've often wondered what makes a person become a policeman, at what point and how they feel that is their vocation. Because, well—'

His wife was more absent than ever. Maigret watched Jean-Claude, who the minute he thought no one was looking at him, scrutinized the inspector closely.

The young man was as cold as the marble of the table. Aged around nineteen or twenty, he already had his father's self-assurance. It would take a lot to shake him, and yet there was a sense of unease about him.

They didn't speak of Monita, who had died the previous week. Perhaps they preferred not to discuss her in front of the butler.

'You see, Maigret,' Malik was saying, 'at school, you were all blind, the lot of you, and you had no idea what you were saying when you called me the Tax Collector. There were a few of us, you remember, who weren't well off, and were more or less excluded by the sons of the local squires and the wealthy. Some boys were upset by this, but others, like you, were indifferent.

'They nicknamed me the Tax Collector out of contempt, and yet that's where my strength lies.

'If you knew everything that passes through a tax collector's hands! I've seen the dirty linen of the outwardly most reputable families . . . I've witnessed the dodgy dealings of those who grew rich. I've seen those who rose up and those who fell, even those who tumbled to the very bottom, and I began to study the way it all worked . . .

'The social mechanism if you like. Why people rise and why they fall.'

He spoke with a scornful pride, in the sumptuous dining room whose decor was reflected in the windows, echoing his success.

'I'm one of the people who rose . . .'

The food was undoubtedly of the highest quality, but Maigret had no liking for those complicated little dishes with sauces invariably studded with truffle shavings or crayfish tails. The butler kept leaning over to fill one of the glasses lined up in front of him.

The sky was turning green on one side, a cold, almost grass green, and red on the other, with purple streaks and scattered clouds of an innocent white. A few canoes lingered on the Seine, where the occasional fish would leap up, making a series of slow loops.

Malik must have had keen hearing, as keen as Maigret, who also heard. And yet it was barely audible, the silence of the evening alone magnified the slightest sound.

A scratching at first, as if at a first-floor window, from the side where, earlier, before dinner, there had been outbursts of shouting. Then a faint thud coming from the garden.

Malik and his son looked at each other. Madame Malik hadn't batted an eyelid but merely carried on raising her fork to her mouth.

Malik whipped off his napkin, put it on the table and raced outside, lithe and silent in his crepe-soled shoes.

The butler seemed no more surprised by this incident than the mistress of the house. But Jean-Claude, on the other hand, had turned slightly red. And now he was casting around for something to say. He opened his mouth and stammered a few words:

'My father is still spry for his age, isn't he?'

With exactly the same smile as his father. In other words:

'Something's going on, obviously, but it's none of your business. Just carry on eating and don't take any notice of the rest.'

'He regularly beats me at tennis, even though I'm not too bad a player. He's an extraordinary man.'

Why did Maigret repeat, staring at his plate:

'Extraordinary . . .'

Someone had been locked in up there, in one of the bedrooms, that was clear. And that someone could not have been happy to be shut up like that, since, before dinner, Malik had had to go upstairs to reprimand him.

That same someone had tried to take advantage of the mealtime, when the entire family was in the dining room, to run away. He had jumped on to the soft flower bed planted with hortensias that surrounded the house.

It was that dull sound of someone landing on the earth that Malik had heard at the same time as Maigret.

And he had raced outside. It must be serious, serious enough to make him behave in a way that was strange, to say the least.

'Does your brother play tennis too?' asked Maigret, looking up and gazing at the young man opposite.

'Why do you ask that? No, my brother isn't sporty.'

'How old is he?'

'Sixteen . . . He's just failed his baccalaureate, and my father is furious.'

'Is that why he locked him in his room?'

'Probably . . . Georges-Henry and my father don't always get along too well.'

'You on the other hand must get along very well with your father, is that right?'

'Fairly well.'

Maigret happened to glance at the hand of the mistress

of the house and was astonished to see that she was gripping her knife so hard that her knuckles had a bluish tinge.

The three of them sat there, waiting, while the butler changed the plates once again. The air was stiller than ever, so still that you could hear the slightest rustle of the leaves in the trees.

When he had regained his footing in the garden, Georges-Henry had set off at a run. In which direction? Not towards the Seine, for he would have been seen. Behind the house, at the bottom of the garden, was the railway line. To the left were the grounds of the Amorelle residence.

The father must be running after his son. And Maigret could not help smiling as he imagined Malik, doubtless driven by rage, forced into this thankless chase.

They had had the cheese, and the dessert. It was the moment when they should have left the table and moved into the drawing room or on to the terrace, where it was still daylight. Glancing at his watch, Maigret saw that it was twelve minutes since the master of the house had rushed outside.

Madame Malik did not rise. Her son was trying discreetly to remind her of her duty when footsteps were heard in the adjacent hall.

It was Malik, with his smile, a slightly tense smile all the same, and the first thing Maigret noticed was that he had changed his trousers. This pair was white flannel too, but clearly fresh out of the wardrobe, the crease still immaculate.

Had Malik got caught in some brambles during his chase? Or had he waded across a stream?

He hadn't had time to go far. His reappearance was still a record, for he was not out of breath, his grey hair had been carefully slicked back, and nothing in his dress was out of place.

'I have a rascal of—'

The son took after his father, for he interrupted him with all the naturalness in the world:

'Georges-Henry again, I'll bet? I was just telling the inspector that he failed his baccalaureate and that you had locked him in his room to make him study.'

Malik didn't falter, showed no satisfaction, no admiration for this adroit rescue. And yet it was a smart move. They had just sent the ball back and forth as deftly as in a game of tennis.

'No thank you, Jean,' said Malik to the butler, who was trying to serve him. 'If madame so wishes, we'll go out on to the terrace.'

Then to his wife:

'Unless you feel tired? . . . In which case my friend Maigret won't be offended if you retire. With your permission, Jules? . . . These past few days have been a great strain for her. She was very fond of her niece.'

What was it that grated? The words were ordinary, the tone banal. And yet Maigret had the sense that he was uncovering, or rather getting a whiff of, something disturbing or menacing behind each sentence.

Erect now in her white dress, Madame Malik gazed at them, and Maigret, without knowing exactly why, would not have been surprised if she had collapsed on the black and white marble floor tiles.

'If you don't mind,' she stammered.

She extended her hand once more, which he brushed and found cold. The three men stepped through the French windows on to the terrace.

'Cigars and brandy, Jean,' ordered the master of the house.

And turning to Maigret, he asked point-blank:

'Are you married?'

'Yes.'

'Children?'

'I have not had that good fortune.'

A curling of Malik's lip that did not escape Jean-Claude, but which didn't shock him.

'Sit down and have a cigar!'

Jean had brought out several boxes, Havana and Manila cigars, several decanters of spirits too, of various shapes.

'The youngest one, you see, is like his grandmother. There's not a hint of Malik about him.'

One thing that hindered the conversation, that irked Maigret, was that he couldn't reconcile himself to the overly familiar tone of his former schoolmate.

'So, Monsieur Malik, did you catch him?' he asked hesitantly.

And Malik misinterpreted his formality. It was fatal. There was a glimmer of satisfaction in his eyes. He clearly thought that the former chief inspector was intimidated by his wealth and did not dare call him by his first name.

'You can call me Ernest,' he said condescendingly, rolling a cigar between his long, manicured fingers. 'We were schoolmates after all . . . No, I didn't catch him and I had no intention of doing so.'

He was lying. It was enough to have seen the way he had raced out of the room.

'I simply wanted to know where he was going . . . He's very highly strung, as sensitive as a girl.

'When I left the room for a moment, earlier, I went up to his room to scold him. I was quite harsh with him and I'm always worried . . .'

Did he read in Maigret's eyes that he was thinking of Monita, making a connection with the girl who had drowned and who was also highly strung? Probably, because he hastened to add:

'Oh! It's not what you think. He loves himself too much to do that! But he does run away sometimes. Once, he went missing for a week and was found by chance on a building site where he had just been hired.'

The eldest boy listened with indifference. He was on his father's side, that was obvious. He had a deep contempt for this brother they were talking about and who took after his grandmother.

'As I knew he had no pocket money, I followed him and I'm relieved . . . He simply went to see old Bernadette and is probably crying on her shoulder as we speak.'

Darkness was falling, and Maigret had the impression that Malik was less concerned about his own facial expressions. His features hardened, his gaze became even sharper, without that irony that tempered its fierceness a little.

'Are you absolutely sure about sleeping at Jeanne's? I could send a servant to go and collect your luggage.'

This insistence displeased Maigret, who interpreted it as a threat. Perhaps he was wrong? Perhaps it was his ill temper counselling him?

'I'll go and sleep at L'Ange,' he said.

'Will you accept my invitation for tomorrow? You'll meet some interesting people here. There aren't many of us. Six houses in total, including the former chateau across the river. But there are some real characters!'

And on that note, a shot was heard coming from the direction of the river. Maigret didn't have a chance to react before his companion explained:

'Old Groux shooting woodpigeon. An eccentric whom you'll meet tomorrow. He owns that entire hill that you can see – or would be able to see if it weren't dark – on the opposite side of the river. He knows I want to buy it, and for twenty years he's been refusing to sell, even though he hasn't got a cent to his name.'

Why had his voice dropped, like someone who is suddenly struck by a new idea mid-sentence?

'Can you find your way back? Jean-Claude will see you to the gate. Will you lock up, Jean-Claude? Follow the towpath and after two hundred metres take the little woodland path that goes straight to L'Ange . . . If you like stories, you'll have your fill, because old Jeanne, who suffers from insomnia, is probably already watching out for you and will give you your money's worth, especially if you sympathize with her woes and take pity on her many ailments.'

He drained his glass and stood up, signalling that the evening was over.

'See you tomorrow, around midday. I'm counting on you.'

He held out a strong, dry hand.

'It's funny bumping into one another after so many years . . . Good night, my friend.'

A slightly patronizing, distant 'goodnight, my friend'.

Already, as Maigret descended the steps accompanied by the eldest son, Malik had vanished inside the house.

There was no moon and the night had grown quite dark. As Maigret walked along the towpath, he heard the slow, repetitive plashing of a pair of oars. A voice hissed:

'Stop!'

The noise ceased, giving way to another, that of a casting net being thrown over the side. Poachers, most likely.

He continued on his way, smoking his pipe, his hands stuffed in his pockets, annoyed with himself and with the others and wondering, in short, what he was doing there instead of being at home.

He passed the wall enclosing the Amorelles' garden. As he walked past the gate, he noticed a light at one of the windows. Now on his left were dark bushes among which, a little further on, he would find the path leading to old Jeanne's place.

Suddenly, there was a sharp snap followed immediately by a faint noise on the ground a few metres ahead of him. He froze, nervous, even though it sounded like the shot earlier, when Malik had told him about an old eccentric who spent his evenings hunting woodpigeon.

All was silent. But there had been someone, not far from

him, probably on the Amorelles' wall, someone who had shot with a rifle and who had not been firing in the air, at some woodpigeon sitting on a branch, but towards the ground, towards Maigret as he walked past.

He scowled, a mix of ill temper and satisfaction. He clenched his fists, furious, and yet he felt relieved. He preferred this.

'Scoundrel!' he grumbled softly.

There was no point in looking for his attacker, in rushing after him as Malik had done earlier. He wouldn't find anything in the dark and he might trip and fall stupidly into a hole.

He kept going, his hands still in his pockets, his pipe between his teeth. His pace did not falter for an instant, his burly frame and deliberately slow tread displaying his contempt.

He reached L'Ange a few minutes later without being used as a target again.

3. Family Portrait in the Drawing Room

It was 9.30 and Maigret was not up yet. For some time now the noises from outside had been filtering in through the wide-open window – the clucking of the hens scratching around in the muck in a courtyard, a dog's chain rattling, the insistent hooting of the tug-boats and the more muffled throbbing of the barge engines.

Maigret had a hangover, and even what he would have called a stinking hangover. Now he knew the secret of old Jeanne, the owner of L'Ange. The previous evening when he'd got back, she'd still been in the dining room, sitting by the clock with the copper pendulum. Malik had been right to warn him that she would be waiting up for him. But it was probably not so much that she wanted to talk, but to drink.

'She can knock it back, all right!' he said to himself, still half-asleep. He didn't dare wake up too abruptly for fear of the thumping headache he knew lay in wait for him.

He should have realized immediately. He had known other women like Jeanne who, after the change of life, have lost all interest in their appearance and drag themselves around, miserable, moaning and groaning, their face shiny and their hair greasy, complaining of every ailment under the sun.

'I'd love a little drink,' he'd said, sitting down beside her, or rather straddling a chair. 'What about you, Madame Jeanne? . . . What can I pour you?'

'Nothing, monsieur. I'd better not drink. Everything's bad for me.'

'A tiny liqueur?'

'All right, just to keep you company . . . A Kummel, then. Would you like to pour one for yourself? . . . The bottles are on the shelf. My legs are very swollen this evening.'

So Kummel was her tipple, that was all. And he too had drunk the caraway-flavoured liqueur out of politeness. He still felt nauseous. He swore he would never touch another drop of Kummel as long as he lived.

How many little glasses had she surreptitiously drained? She talked, in her complaining voice at first, and then becoming more animated. From time to time, looking elsewhere, she would grab the bottle and pour herself a glass. Until Maigret caught on and found himself refilling his glass every ten minutes.

Strange evening. The maid had long since gone to bed. The cat was curled up in Madame Jeanne's lap, the pendulum swung to and fro behind the glass door of the grandfather clock, and the woman talked, first of all about Marius, her deceased husband, and then about herself, a girl from a good family who had followed Marius and missed out on marrying an officer who had since become a general.

'He came here with his wife and children, three years ago now, a few days before Marius died. He didn't recognize me.'

About Bernadette Amorelle:

'They say she's mad, but it isn't true. It's just that she's got a peculiar nature. Her husband was a great brute. It was he who founded the big Seine quarries.'

Madame Jeanne was no fool.

'I know why you've come here, now . . . Everyone knows . . . I think you're wasting your time.'

She was talking about the Maliks, Ernest and Charles.

'You haven't seen Charles yet? You'll meet him . . . and his wife, the youngest of the Amorelle girls, Mademoiselle Aimée as she used to be called. You'll meet them. We are a tiny village, aren't we? Not even a hamlet. And yet strange things happen here. Yes, Mademoiselle Monita was found at the weir.'

No, she, Madame Jeanne, didn't know anything. Can one ever know what goes on inside a young girl's head?

She drank, Maigret drank, listened to her chatter and refilled the glasses, feeling as if he had been bewitched, and saying from time to time:

'I'm keeping you up.'

'Oh you don't need to worry about me. I don't sleep very much, with all my aches and pains! But if you're tired . . .'

He stayed a while longer. And, when they each went up separate staircases, he had heard a clatter as Madame Jeanne fell down the stairs.

She couldn't be up yet. He resolved to get out of bed and to go into the bathroom, first to drink, to drink great gulps of cold water, then to wash off his sweat smelling of alcohol, of Kummel. No! Never again would he touch a glass of Kummel.

Well well! Someone had just arrived at the inn. He could hear the maid's voice saying:

'He's still asleep, I tell you . . .'

He leaned out of the window and saw a maid in a black dress and white apron talking to Raymonde.

'Is it for me?' he asked.

And looking up, the maid said:

'You can see perfectly well that he's not asleep!'

She was holding a letter, an envelope with a black border, and she stated:

'I'm to wait for a reply.'

Raymonde brought up the letter. He had put his trousers on, and his braces dangled against his thighs. It was already hot. A fine haze rose from the river.

Will you come and see me as soon as possible? It is best for you to follow my maid, who will show you the way to my apartment, otherwise you will not be allowed up. I know you are meeting them all at lunch time.

  Bernadette Amorelle

He followed the maid, who was in her forties and very ugly, with the same beady eyes as her mistress. She did not utter a word and her body language seemed to be saying: 'No point trying to get me to talk. I have my instructions and I won't let myself be pushed around.'

They followed the wall, went through the gate and walked up the drive leading to the vast Amorelle residence. Birds were singing in all the trees. The gardener was pushing a wheelbarrow full of manure.

The house was less modern than that of Ernest Malik, less sumptuous, as if already dimmed by the mists of time.

'This way . . .'

They did not enter through the big main door at the top of the steps, but through a little door in the east wing. They climbed a staircase whose walls were hung with nineteenth-century prints and had not yet reached the landing when a door opened and Madame Amorelle appeared, as erect, as imperious as on the previous day.

'You took your time,' she declared.

'The gentleman wasn't ready . . . I had to wait while he got dressed.'

'This way, inspector. I would have thought that a man like you would be an early riser.'

It was her bedroom, a vast room, with three windows. The four-poster bed was already made. There were objects lying around on the furniture, giving the impression that the elderly lady lived her entire life in this room, which was her exclusive preserve, whose door she was reluctant to open.

'Sit down. Please . . . I hate talking to someone who remains standing. You may smoke your pipe, if you need to. My husband smoked his pipe all day long. The smell is not as bad as cigar smoke . . . So, you had dinner at my son-in-law's?'

Maigret might have found it amusing to hear himself being treated like a little boy, but that morning, his sense of humour had deserted him.

'I did indeed have dinner with Ernest Malik,' he said gruffly.

'What did he tell you?'

'That you were a mad old woman and that his son Georges-Henry was nearly as mad as you.'

'Did you believe him?'

'Then, when I was on my way back to L'Ange, someone, who probably deems my career has been long enough, took a pot-shot at me. I suppose that the young man was here?'

'Which young man? ... You mean Georges-Henry? I didn't see him all evening.'

'And yet his father claimed that he was sheltering here—'

'If you take everything he says as gospel—'

'You haven't heard from him?'

'Not at all, and I'd be very happy to. In short, what did you find out?'

Just then he looked at her and wondered, without knowing why, whether she really wanted him to have found out something.

'You seem to be getting on famously with my son-in-law Ernest,' she went on.

'We were in the same class at school in Moulins, and he insists on calling me by my first name, as if we were still twelve years old.'

He was in a foul mood. His head hurt. His pipe tasted stale and he had been obliged to leave and follow the maid without drinking his coffee, because there was none ready at L'Ange.

He was beginning to tire of this family where people all spied on one another and nobody seemed to be speaking the truth.

'I fear for Georges-Henry,' she was murmuring now. 'He

was so fond of his cousin. I wouldn't be surprised if there had been something between them.'

'He's sixteen.'

She looked him up and down.

'And do you think that makes any difference? . . . I was never so much in love as I was at sixteen and, were I to have done something stupid, it is at that age that I would have done it. You'd do well to find Georges-Henry.'

And he, frosty, almost sarcastic:

'Where do you suggest I look?'

'That's your job, not mine. I wonder why his father claimed he had seen him coming here. Malik knows very well that's not true.'

Her voice betrayed a genuine concern. She paced up and down the room, but each time Maigret made to get to his feet, she repeated:

'Sit down.'

She spoke as if to herself.

'They've arranged a big luncheon today. Charles Malik and his wife will be there. They have also invited old Campois and that old stick-in-the-mud Groux. I received an invitation too, first thing this morning. I wonder if Georges-Henry will be back.'

'You have nothing else to tell me, madame?'

'What does that mean?'

'Nothing. When you came to Meung yesterday, you hinted that you refused to believe that your granddaughter had died a natural death.'

She stared hard at him, without revealing anything of her thoughts.

'And now that you're here,' she retorted with a note of anger, 'are you going to tell me that you find what's going on natural?'

'I didn't say that.'

'Well! Go ahead. Go to this luncheon.'

'Will you be there?'

'I don't know. Keep your eyes and ears open. And, if you are as good as they say you are . . .'

She was displeased with him, that was clear. Was he not being flexible enough, respectful enough of her idiosyncrasies? Was she disappointed that he hadn't uncovered anything yet?

She was on edge and anxious, despite her self-control. She headed for the door, thus dismissing him.

'I'm afraid those scoundrels really are cleverer than you!' she said by way of a parting shot. 'We'll see. Right now, I'll wager anything you like that they are all downstairs waiting for you.'

It was true. As he stepped into the corridor, a door opened noiselessly. A maid – not the same one who had brought him here – said deferentially:

'Monsieur and Madame Malik are waiting for you in the morning room. If you would be so good as to follow me . . .'

The house was cool, the walls painted with faded colours and everywhere were carved doors, overmantels, paintings and engravings. Soft carpets muffled footsteps and the Venetian blinds let in just enough light.

One last door. He took two steps forwards and found

himself facing Monsieur and Madame Malik in full mourning, waiting for him.

What was it that gave him the impression not of reality, but of a carefully composed family portrait? He did not yet know Charles Malik, in whom he found none of his brother's features, even though there was a family resemblance. He was a little younger, more corpulent. His ruddy face was pinker, and his eyes were not grey like Ernest's, but an almost innocent blue.

Nor did he have his brother's assurance, and there were dark circles under his eyes, a certain flabbiness about his lips, an anxious look in his eyes.

He stood very upright in front of the marble fireplace, and his wife was seated close to him in a Louis XVI armchair, her hands in her lap, as for a photograph.

The entire scene exuded sorrow, overwhelming grief even. Charles Malik spoke in a faltering voice.

'Do come in, inspector, and please forgive us for having asked you to drop in to see us for a moment.'

As for Madame Malik, she looked very much like her sister, but was more refined, with something of her mother's vivacity. That vivacity, at present, was as if shrouded – understandably, given her recent bereavement. In her right hand she held a little handkerchief screwed into a ball, which she scrunched constantly during their conversation.

'Do please sit down. I know that we will be meeting each other later on at my brother's house. Myself in any case, for I doubt my wife feels up to attending this luncheon.

I don't know under what circumstances you came here and I should like—'

He looked at his wife, who merely gazed at him with simplicity but determination.

'This is a very difficult time for us, inspector, and my mother-in-law's obstinacy bodes even worse to come. You've met her. I don't know what you make of her.'

Maigret, in any case, took good care not to tell him, because he sensed that Charles Malik was beginning to flounder and was summoning his wife to his aid once more.

'Remember, Mother is eighty-two years old,' she said. 'It's all too easy to forget because she has so much energy . . . Sadly, her mind isn't always as alert as her body. She's completely devastated by the death of my daughter, who was her favourite.'

'I appreciate that, madame.'

'You can see, now, the atmosphere we have been living in since the tragedy. Mother has got it into her head that there is some mystery behind it.'

'The inspector has certainly gathered that,' continued Charles Malik. 'Don't get upset, darling . . . My wife is very highly strung, inspector. We all are at the moment. Our affection for my mother-in-law alone is stopping us from taking the steps that would seem necessary. That is why we are asking you . . .'

Maigret pricked up his ears.

'. . . we are asking you . . . to carefully weigh up the pros and cons before—'

Goodness! Could it have been this bumbling, tubby man who had fired at Maigret the previous evening? There was nothing implausible about this notion that had just occurred to him.

Ernest Malik was a cold-blooded animal and most likely, if he had fired, he would have aimed more accurately. Whereas Charles, on the other hand . . .

'I understand your situation,' continued the master of the house, leaning on the mantelpiece in a more family-portrait pose than ever. 'It is delicate, very delicate. In short—'

'In short,' broke in Maigret, in his most ingratiating tone, 'I wonder what on earth I'm doing here.'

He covertly watched Charles Malik and caught his little tremor of delight.

That was exactly what they had wanted him to say. What was he doing there, in fact? No one had invited him, other than an old woman of eighty-two who wasn't completely compos mentis.

'I wouldn't go so far as to say that,' Charles Malik corrected him, very much the gentleman, 'given that you are a friend of Ernest's, I think it would be better—'

'Tell me.'

'Yes . . . I think it would be fitting, or rather desirable, that you do not overly encourage my mother-in-law in these ideas which . . . that—'

'You are convinced, Monsieur Malik, that your daughter's death was absolutely natural?'

'I think it was an accident.'

He was blushing, but had replied firmly.

'And what about you, madame?'

The handkerchief was just a tiny ball in her hand.

'I think the same as my husband.'

'In that case, clearly . . .'

He was giving them hope. He could sense them swelling with the hope that they were going to be forever rid of his burdensome presence.

'. . . I am obliged to accept your brother's invitation. Then, if nothing happens, if no new developments require my presence . . .'

He rose, almost as ill-at-ease as they were. He was eager to be outside, to take a deep breath of fresh air.

'So I'll see you in a little while,' Charles Malik was saying. 'I apologize for not showing you out, but I still have things to do.'

'Don't mention it. My humble respects, madame.'

He was still in the grounds, walking down towards the Seine, when he was struck by a noise. It was that of the handle of a rural telephone turning, with the short ring signalling that the call had been heard.

'He has telephoned his brother to report back to him,' thought Maigret.

And he believed he could guess what was being said:

'Phew! He's leaving. He promised. As long as nothing happens at lunch.'

A tug-boat was pulling its eight barges towards the Haute Seine, and it was a tug-boat with a green triangle, an Amorelle and Campois tug-boat; the barges were also Amorelle and Campois.

It was only half past eleven. He couldn't face going to L'Ange, where there was nothing for him to do. He walked along the riverbank mulling over his confused thoughts. He paused like a sightseer in front of Ernest Malik's luxury pontoon. He had his back to the Maliks' residence.

'Well! Maigret?'

It was Ernest Malik, dressed this time in a grey salt-and-pepper suit and wearing white kid shoes and a panama hat.

'My brother has just telephoned me.'

'I know.'

'Apparently you have already had enough of my mother-in-law's nonsense.'

There was something suppressed in his voice, something emphatic in his eyes.

'If I understand correctly, you want to get back to your wife and your lettuce patch?'

Then, without knowing why (perhaps that is what is known as inspiration), Maigret, making himself heavier, thicker, more inert than ever, replied:

'No.'

Malik reacted. Despite all his sang-froid, he could not help himself. For a moment, he looked like someone trying to swallow his saliva, and his Adam's apple visibly rose and fell two or three times.

'Ah! . . .'

A brief glance about them, but he wasn't planning to push Maigret into the Seine.

'We still have a good while ahead of us before the guests arrive. We usually lunch late. Come into my study for a moment.'

Not a word was spoken as they crossed the grounds.

Maigret glimpsed Madame Malik arranging flowers in the vases in the drawing room.

They skirted the house, and Malik walked ahead of his guest into a fairly vast study, with deep leather armchairs and walls decorated with model ships.

'You may smoke.'

He carefully shut the door and half-lowered the Venetian blinds, because the sun was streaming into the room. At last he sat down at his desk and started fiddling with a crystal paper knife.

Maigret had perched on the arm of an armchair and was slowly filling his pipe, giving the impression that his mind was a blank. When the silence had gone on for some time, he asked quietly:

'Where is your son?'

'Which one?'

Then, correcting himself:

'This is not about my son.'

'It's about me, isn't it?'

'What do you mean?'

'Nothing.'

'Well! Yes, it is about you.'

Beside this wiry, elegant man with refined, well-groomed features, Maigret cut an oafish figure.

'How much are you offering me?'

'What makes you think that I was planning to offer you anything?'

'I imagine you are.'

'Why not, after all? The police force isn't very generous. I don't know what kind of a pension they pay you.'

And Maigret, still gentle and humble:

'Three thousand, two hundred.'

He added, with disarming candour:

'Of course, we have some savings.'

This time, Ernest Malik was truly disconcerted. This seemed all too easy. He had the feeling his former school-mate was laughing at him. And yet . . .

'Listen—'

'I'm all ears—'

'I know what you're going to think.'

'I think so little!'

'You're going to think that your presence here bothers me, that I have something to hide. And supposing that were the case?'

'Yes, supposing that were the case? It's none of my business, is it?'

'Are you being sarcastic?'

'Never.'

'You'd be wasting your time with me, you see. You probably think you're very clever. You have had a successful and distinguished career chasing thieves and murderers. Well, Jules my friend, there are no thieves or murderers here. Do you understand? Through the greatest of coincidences, you have landed in a world you don't know and where you are likely to do a lot of damage. That's why I'm telling you—'

'How much?'

'A hundred thousand.'

Maigret didn't bat an eyelid, then Malik said, nodding hesitantly:

'A hundred and fifty. I'll go up to two hundred thousand.'

He was on his feet now, jittery, tense, still fiddling with the paper knife, which suddenly snapped between his fingers. A bead of blood formed on his index finger and Maigret commented:

'You've hurt yourself.'

'Be quiet. Or rather answer my question. I'll write out a cheque for two hundred thousand francs. Not a cheque? No matter . . . The car will take us to Paris later and I'll pick up the cash from my bank. Then I'll drive you back to Meung.'

Maigret sighed.

'What's your answer?'

'Where is your son?'

This time, Malik could not contain his anger.

'It's none of your business. It's no one's business, do you hear? I'm not in your office at Quai des Orfèvres and neither are you. I am asking you to leave because your presence here is ill-timed, to say the least. People are talking. They're wondering—'

'What exactly are they wondering?'

'One last time, I'm asking you politely to leave. And if you do, I'm prepared to offer you a very generous reward. Is it yes or is it no?'

'It's no, of course.'

'Very well. In that case, I'm going to have to change my tune.'

'Go ahead.'

'I'm no angel and I never was. Otherwise I wouldn't be where I am today. Now, through your pig-headedness, through your stupidity, yes, stupidity, you're likely to unleash a calamity that you don't even suspect. And you're happy, aren't you? You think you're still in the Police Judiciaire grilling some little cutthroat or some young delinquent who's strangled an old woman.

'I haven't strangled anyone, you should know that. I haven't robbed anyone either.'

'In that case—'

'Silence! You want to stay, so you'll stay. You'll carry on poking your big nose in everywhere. Well, on your head be it.

'You see, Maigret, I'm a lot stronger than you are and I've proved it.

'If I'd been made of the same stuff as you, I'd have become a good little income-tax collector like my father.

'Meddle in what doesn't concern you if you must!

'On your head be it.'

He had regained his outer calm and his lips were again curled in a sneer.

Maigret, who had risen, was looking around for his hat.

'Where are you going?'

'Outside.'

'Aren't you having lunch with us?'

'I'd rather lunch elsewhere.'

'As you wish. And there again, you're being petty. Petty and narrow-minded.'

'Is that all?'

'For now, yes.'

And, hat in hand, Maigret strode calmly over to the door. He opened it and went out, without looking back. Outside, a shape darted off, and he just had the time to recognize Jean-Claude, the eldest son, who must have been eavesdropping beneath the open window and had overheard the entire conversation.

He walked around the house and, in the main drive, passed two men whom he hadn't yet met.

One was short and stocky with a thick neck and big, coarse hands: Monsieur Campois probably, for he matched the description Jeanne had given him the previous evening. The other, who must have been his grandson, was a strapping boy with an open face.

They stared at him in bewilderment, as he made his way calmly towards the gate, then they both turned around to look at him, stopping even to watch him.

'That's one thing out of the way!' said Maigret to himself as he walked off along the towpath.

A boat was crossing the river, steered by an old man in a yellowish linen suit, with a splendid red tie. It was Monsieur Groux, on his way to the gathering. They would all be there, except him, for whose benefit this lunch had been arranged in the first place.

What about Georges-Henry? Maigret began to move faster. He wasn't hungry, but he was terribly thirsty. In any case, he swore to himself again that, whatever happened, he would drink no more little tipples of Kummel with old Jeanne.

When he walked into L'Ange, he did not see the owner in her usual place by the grandfather clock. He poked his head around the half-open kitchen door and Raymonde called out:

'I thought you weren't having lunch here?'

Then, raising her plump arms to the heavens:

'I haven't cooked anything. Madame is unwell and doesn't want to come downstairs.'

There wasn't even any beer in the house.

4. The Top Kennel

It would have been hard to say how it happened: the fact was that Maigret and Raymonde were now friends. Only an hour ago, she was sorely tempted to ban him from entering her kitchen.

'I have nothing to eat, I tell you.'

What's more, she didn't like men. She found them violent and they smelled unpleasant. Most of the men who came to L'Ange, even the married ones, tried to grope her and it disgusted her.

She had wanted to become a nun. She was tall and languid despite her apparent energy.

'What are you after?' she asked impatiently, seeing Maigret standing in front of the open larder.

'A little leftover something-or-other. Anything. It's so hot that I haven't got the energy to go and eat up at the lock.'

'Well, there aren't any leftovers here! First of all, in theory, the place is closed. As a matter of fact, it's up for sale. Has been for three years. And each time the sale is about to go through, the old lady wavers, finds reasons to object and ends up saying no. She doesn't need to make her living from it, does she!'

'What about you, what are you going to eat?'

'Bread and cheese.'

'Do you not think there'll be enough for the two of us?'

He looked kind, with his slightly flushed face and his round eyes. He had made himself at home in the kitchen and ignored Raymonde when she said:

'Get out of here, it hasn't been cleaned yet. I'll lay you a place in the dining room.'

He had dug his heels in.

'I'll go and see if there isn't a tin of sardines left, but it'll be lucky if there is. There are no shops around here. The butcher, the *charcuterie* and even the grocer from Corbeil come and deliver to the big houses, the Maliks, the Campois. Before, they used to stop here and we were able to stock up. But the old lady barely eats a thing nowadays and she thinks that others should do likewise. Wait, let me go and see if there are any eggs in the hen house.'

There were three. Maigret insisted on making the omelette, and she laughed as she watched him whisk the egg yolks and whites separately.

'Why didn't you go and have lunch at the Maliks', seeing as you're invited? I hear their cook used to be chef to the king of Norway or Sweden, I don't remember which.'

'I'd rather stay here and have a bite to eat with you.'

'In the kitchen! With no tablecloth!'

Yet it was true. And Raymonde, unwittingly, was providing him with invaluable help. He felt relaxed here. He had removed his jacket and rolled up his shirt-sleeves. From time to time, he got up to pour boiling water over the coffee.

'I wonder what keeps her here,' Raymonde had said, among other things, talking about old Jeanne. 'She's got more money than she'll ever spend, no children and no heirs, since she booted her nephews out a long time ago.'

It was insights like that which, added to memories of the previous evening, to insignificant details, helped flesh out for Maigret a solid picture of the inn owner's character.

She had once been beautiful, Raymonde also told him. And it was true. You could tell, even though she was over fifty, despite her ill-kempt look, her lank, greasy hair and her sallow complexion.

A woman who had been beautiful and was intelligent, but who had suddenly let herself go, who drank, who lived a fiercely reclusive existence, complaining and drinking to the point of taking to her bed for days on end.

'She'll never make up her mind to leave Orsenne.'

Well! By the time all the characters had taken on the same human roundness, when he could 'feel' them the way he could feel the owner of L'Ange, the mystery would be very close to being solved.

There was Bernadette Amorelle, whom he was close to understanding.

'Old Monsieur Amorelle, who died, wasn't at all like his sons-in-law. More like Monsieur Campois. I don't know if you see what I mean. He was tough, but fair. He would go down to the lock to chat with his bargemen and he wasn't too proud to sit and have a drink with them.'

In other words, they were the first generation who'd done well for themselves, with their big, unpretentious houses.

Then the next generation, the two daughters who had

married the Malik brothers, the modern residence, the pontoon, the luxury cars.

'Tell me, Raymonde, did you know Monita well?'

'Of course I did. I knew her when she was a little girl, because I've been at L'Ange for seven years and, seven years ago, she'd just turned ten. A right tomboy ... She was always giving her governess the slip and they'd go hunting all over the place for her. Sometimes all the servants would be sent along the towpath calling Monita. She had usually run off with her cousin Georges-Henry.'

Maigret had never set eyes on him either. He had heard people describe him.

'He wasn't all dressed up to the nines like his brother! Nearly always in shorts, and rather grubby shorts at that, with his bare legs and tousled hair. He was terrified of his father!'

'Were Monita and Georges-Henry in love?'

'I don't know whether Monita was in love. A woman hides her feelings better. But he definitely was.'

It was peaceful in this kitchen where only a single slanting ray of sunshine filtered in. Maigret smoked his pipe, his elbows on the polished heavy timber table, and sipped his coffee.

'Have you seen him since his cousin's death?'

'I saw him at the funeral. He was very pale, red-eyed. Right in the middle of the service, he started sobbing. At the cemetery, when people were filing past the open grave, he suddenly began grabbing the flowers by the handful and throwing them on to the coffin.'

'And since?'

'I think they're keeping him locked up inside the house.'

She stared at Maigret inquisitively. She had heard that he was a famous policeman, that during his career he had arrested hundreds of criminals and solved the most complicated cases. And this man was here in her kitchen, dressed casually, smoking his pipe and talking to her informally, asking her mundane questions.

What could he be hoping for? She felt something akin to pity for him. He was probably getting old, because they'd retired him.

'Now, I must wash my dishes, then I've got to mop the floor.'

He didn't leave and his face was still as placid, as if devoid of thought.

'In short,' he muttered suddenly, 'Monita is dead and Georges-Henry has gone.'

She looked up abruptly.

'Are you sure he has gone?'

And he rose, his attitude now hardened, displaying a sudden determination.

'Listen to me for a moment, Raymonde. Hold on. Give me a pencil and a piece of paper.'

She tore a page from a grease-stained notebook in which she kept her accounts. She did not understand what he was leading up to.

'Yesterday . . . Let's see . . . We were on the cheese. So it was around nine o'clock in the evening . . . Georges-Henry jumped out of his bedroom window and ran off.'

'In which direction?'

'Off to the right. If he had gone down to the Seine, I

would have seen him running across the garden. If he had gone to the left, I would also have seen him because the dining room has windows on both sides. Hold on . . . His father ran after him. Ernest Malik stayed away for twelve minutes. It's true that during those twelve minutes he took the time to change his trousers and run a comb through his hair. To do that, he must have gone up to his bedroom. At least three or four minutes. Now, you know the area well, think carefully before you reply. Which way could Georges-Henry have gone if he had intended to leave Orsenne?'

'To the right is his grandmother and his uncle's house,' she said, looking at the rough sketch he was drawing as she spoke. 'There's no wall between the two gardens but a hedge that has a couple of gaps in it.'

'And then?'

'From the neighbouring garden he would have been able to reach the little path that goes to the station.'

'You can't turn off the path before the station?'

'No . . . Or perhaps he took a boat across the river.'

'Is there a way out from the bottom of the garden?'

'Only with a ladder. Both the Amorelles and the Maliks have a wall that's too high to climb over. The railway line runs past the end of both gardens.'

'Another question. When I came back an hour later, there was a boat on the water. I heard someone casting a fishing net.'

'That's Alphonse, the lock-keeper's son.'

'Thank you, Raymonde. If you don't mind, we'll have dinner together.'

'But there's nothing to eat.'

'There's a grocer's next to the lock. I'll buy the necessaries.'

He was pleased with himself. He had the sense of having set foot on dry land again, and Raymonde watched him lumber off in the direction of the lock. The weir was around five hundred metres away. There were no boats in the lock, and the lock-keeper was sitting on his blue-stone doorstep whittling a piece of wood for one of his kids, while in the gloomy kitchen a woman came and went, a baby in her arms.

'Tell me . . .' ventured Maigret.

The man had jumped to his feet and touched his cap.

'You've come about the young lady, haven't you?'

The local people already knew who he was. Everyone was aware of his presence.

'Well, yes and no . . . I don't suppose you know anything about her?'

'Except that I was the one who found her. Over there, on the third section of the weir. It was a terrible shock, because we knew her well. She often used to come through the lock in her canoe on the way down to Corbeil.'

'Was your son out on the water last night?'

The man looked uncomfortable.

'Don't worry, I'm not interested in poachers. I spotted him at around ten o'clock, but I'd like to know whether he was already out an hour earlier.'

'He'll tell you himself. You'll find him in his workshop, a hundred metres further down. He's the boat builder.'

A wooden shed where two men were busy finishing off a flat-bottomed fishing boat.

'I was on the water with Albert, yes . . . He's my apprentice. First of all we put out the creels, then when we came back—'

'If someone had crossed the river by boat between the Maliks' house and the lock at around nine o'clock, would you have seen them?'

'Definitely. First of all, it wasn't dark yet. Then, even if we hadn't seen him, we'd have heard him. When you fish the way we do, you keep your ears pricked and . . .'

In the little grocer's shop where the bargemen stocked up, Maigret bought some tinned food, eggs, cheese and sausage.

'I can tell that you're at L'Ange!' commented the shopkeeper. 'There's never anything to eat there. They'd do better to close down for good.'

Maigret walked up to the station. It was merely a halt with a crossing-keeper's cottage.

'No, monsieur, nobody came by around that time last night, or up to ten thirty. I was sitting on a chair in front of the house with my wife. Monsieur Georges-Henry? Definitely not him. We know him well and besides, he would have stopped for a chat, because he knows us too and he's not stuck-up.'

But Maigret persisted. He peered over the hedges, chatted to good people out gardening, nearly all of them retired.

'Monsieur Georges-Henry? No, we haven't seen him. Has something happened to him too?'

A big car drove past. It was Ernest Malik's, but it wasn't him at the wheel, it was his brother Charles, heading in the direction of Paris.

It was seven o'clock by the time Maigret got back to L'Ange. Raymonde burst out laughing as he emptied his pockets, which were bulging with provisions.

'With all that, we'll be able to have a bite to eat,' she said.

'Is Madame Jeanne still in bed? Has no one been to see her?'

Raymonde hesitated for a moment.

'Monsieur Malik came earlier. When I told him that you'd gone to the lock, he went upstairs. The two of them were up there whispering for a quarter of an hour, but I couldn't hear what they were saying.'

'Does he often come and see Jeanne?'

'He drops in occasionally. You don't have any news of Georges-Henry?'

Maigret went into the garden to smoke a pipe until dinner was ready. Bernadette Amorelle seemed to have been speaking the truth when she told him that she hadn't seen her grandson. True, that proved nothing. Maigret was close to believing that they were all lying, every single one of them.

And yet he felt that she had been telling the truth.

There was something in Orsenne, something in the Malik family, that had to be hushed up at all costs. Was it in some way connected with Monita's death? Possibly, but it wasn't certain.

The fact was that two people had broken away. First of all, old Madame Amorelle had taken advantage of her daughter and son-in-law's absence to be driven to Meung in the old-fashioned limousine to summon Maigret to the rescue.

Then, on the same day, when the former inspector happened to be in Ernest Malik's house, there had been a second escape. This time, it was Georges-Henry.

Why had his father claimed that the young man was at his grandmother's? Why, in that case, had he not taken him there? And why had he not seen him again the next day?

All that was still unclear, for sure. Ernest Malik had been right when he had looked at Maigret with a smile that was a mixture of sarcasm and contempt. This wasn't a case for him. He was out of his depth. This world was unfamiliar to him, and he had difficulty piecing it all together. Even the decor shocked him for its artificiality. Those huge mansions with deserted gardens and closed blinds, those gardeners trundling up and down the paths, that pontoon, those tiny, heavily lacquered boats, those gleaming cars sitting in garages . . .

And these people who stuck together, these brothers and sisters-in-law who loathed each other perhaps, but who warned each other of danger and closed ranks against him.

What was more, they were in deep mourning. They had on their side the dignity of bereavement and grief. In what capacity, what right did he have to come sniffing around here and poking his nose into their business?

He had almost given up earlier, just as he was returning to L'Ange for lunch, to be exact. What had stopped him had been Raymonde, who had been so easy to win over, and the relaxed, messy atmosphere of the kitchen. It was the words she had inadvertently let slip, her elbows casually on the table, that had lodged in his mind.

She had spoken of Monita, who was a tomboy and who kept running away with her cousin. Of Georges-Henry with his grubby shorts and unkempt hair.

Now Monita was dead and Georges-Henry had disappeared.

He would seek and he would find. That, at least, was his profession. He had been all around Orsenne. He was now almost certain that the young man had not left. At least he was pretty sure that he had lain low somewhere until nightfall and that then he had been able to remain unseen.

Maigret ate voraciously, in the kitchen again, just him and Raymonde.

'If Madame were to see us, she wouldn't like it,' said Raymonde. 'She asked me earlier what you'd eaten. I told her that I served you two fried eggs in the dining room. She also asked me whether you'd mentioned leaving.'

'Before or after Malik's visit?'

'After.'

'In that case, I'll wager that tomorrow she'll refuse to come down from her room again.'

'She came down earlier. I didn't see her. I was at the bottom of the garden. But I noticed that she'd been down.'

He smiled. He had understood. He pictured Jeanne descending noiselessly, having watched her housemaid go out, to come and get a bottle from the shelf!

'I may be back late,' he announced.

'Have they invited you again?'

'No, but I feel like going out for a stroll.'

At first he stayed on the towpath waiting for nightfall. Then he headed for the level crossing, where he saw the keeper, in the shadows, sitting outside his cottage, smoking a long-stemmed pipe.

'Do you mind if I take a walk beside the railway track?'

'Dear me, it's against the regulations, but seeing as you're from the police … Keep a lookout for the train that comes by at seventeen minutes past ten.'

Three hundred metres further on he caught sight of the wall of the first property, that of Madame Amorelle and Charles Malik. It wasn't completely dark yet, but inside the houses, the lamps had long been lit.

There was light on the ground floor. One of the first-floor windows, one of the old lady's bedroom windows, was wide open, and it was rather strange to peep into a private world from a distance, through the blue-tinged air and the tranquillity of the garden, and discover an apartment whose furniture and objects seemed to be frozen in a yellowish light.

He paused for a few moments to watch. A shadow crossed his field of vision. It was not that of Bernadette, but of her daughter, Charles' wife, who was pacing up and down anxiously and seemed to be speaking emphatically.

The old lady must be in her armchair, or her bed, or in one of the corners of the bedroom that was hidden from his view.

He continued along the railway track and came to the second garden, that of Ernest Malik. It was less bushy and had more open space, with wide, well-maintained paths. Here too, lamps were on, but the light only filtered through the blinds and Maigret wasn't able to see inside.

He stood looking down into the garden itself, where,

camouflaged by the young hazelnut trees planted along the railway line, Maigret could make out two tall shapes, pale and silent, and he remembered the Great Danes that had bounded over to lick their master's hand the day before.

They were probably let loose every night, and were likely to be ferocious.

To the right, at the end of the garden, stood a little cottage which Maigret had not yet seen and which was probably where the gardeners and the driver lived.

There was a light on there too, a single one, which went out half an hour later.

There was no sign of the moon yet, but the night was not as dark as the previous one. Maigret sat down quietly on the embankment, facing the hazelnut trees which concealed him, and which he could draw aside with his hand like a curtain.

The 10.17 train sped past less than three metres from him and he watched its red lamp disappear around the bend in the track.

The few lights from Orsenne went out one by one. Old Groux was probably not out hunting woodpigeon that night, since the peace and quiet wasn't shattered by any gunshots.

At last, at nearly eleven o'clock, the two dogs, lying side by side at the edge of a lawn, rose as one and loped towards the house.

They vanished for a moment behind it, and, when Maigret saw them again, the two animals were prancing around the shape of a man who was walking hurriedly and seemed to be making straight for him.

It was Ernest Malik, without a doubt. The shape was too slim and too energetic to be that of one of the servants. He walked silently across the lawn. In his hand he had an object that it was impossible to identify, but which looked quite bulky.

For a good while, Maigret wondered where on earth Malik could be going. He saw him suddenly veer to the right and come so close to the wall that he could hear the dogs' panting.

'Quiet, Satan . . . Quiet, Lionne.'

There, between the trees, was a little brick building that must have pre-dated the house, a low building covered in ancient tiles. Former stables perhaps, or a kennel?

'A kennel,' Maigret said to himself. 'He's simply feeding the dogs.'

But no! Malik pushed the dogs away, took a key out of his pocket, and went inside the building. The key could clearly be heard turning in the lock. Then there was silence, a very long silence, during which Maigret's pipe went out, but he didn't dare re-light it.

Half an hour went by, and finally Malik emerged and locked the door carefully behind him. Then, after looking around cautiously, he strode rapidly towards the house.

At eleven thirty, everything was asleep or seemed to be asleep. When Maigret walked past the back of the Amorelles' garden, he noticed only a tiny night-light burning in old Bernadette's room.

No lights on at L'Ange either. He was wondering how he would get in when the door opened noiselessly. He saw or rather sensed Raymonde, who stood there in her night-dress and slippers. She put her finger on her lips and whispered:

'Go upstairs quickly. Don't make a noise. She didn't want me to leave the door unlocked.'

He would have liked to linger, to ask her a few questions and have something to drink, but a creaking sound coming from Jeanne's room alarmed the girl, who rushed up the stairs.

Then he stood still for a good while. A smell of fried eggs hung in the air, with a whiff of alcohol. Why not? He struck a match, took a bottle from the shelf and tucked it under his arm to go upstairs to bed.

Old Jeanne was shuffling around in her room. She must know that he was back. But he had no wish to go and keep her company.

He took off his jacket, his collar and his tie and undid his braces, letting them dangle down his back and then, in his tooth mug, mixed brandy and water.

One last pipe, leaning on the window-sill, absently contemplating the gently rustling foliage.

He awoke at seven to the sound of Raymonde bustling about in the kitchen. With his pipe in his mouth – the first pipe, the best – he went downstairs and boomed a cheerful 'Good morning'.

'Tell me, Raymonde, you who know every house around here—'

'I do and I don't.'

'Fine. At the bottom of Ernest Malik's garden, on one side there's the gardeners' cottage.'

'Yes. The driver and the servants sleep there too. Not the maids. They sleep in the house.'

'But what about on the other side, close to the railway embankment?'

'There's nothing.'

'There's a very low building. A sort of elongated hut.'

'The top kennel,' she said.

'What's the top kennel?'

'In the old days, long before I came here, the two gardens were one. It was the Amorelles' estate. Old Amorelle was a hunter. There were two kennels, the bottom one, as it was called, for the guard dogs, and the top one for the hunting hounds.'

'Doesn't Ernest Malik hunt?'

'Not here, there isn't enough game for him. He has a house and dogs in Sologne.'

But something was bothering him.

'Is the building in good repair?'

'I don't remember. I haven't been in the garden for a long time. There was a cellar where—'

'Are you certain there was a cellar?'

'There used to be one, in any case. I know because people used to say that there was a hidden treasure in the garden. Before Monsieur Amorelle built his place, forty years ago, or perhaps more, there was already a sort of little ruined chateau. It was rumoured that at the time of the Revolution, the people from the chateau hid their valuables somewhere in the grounds. At one point, Monsieur Amorelle tried to find it and called in water diviners. They all said that the search should focus on the cellar of the top kennel.

'None of that is of any importance,' muttered Maigret. 'What matters is that there is a cellar. And it is in that cellar, my dear Raymonde, that poor Georges-Henry must be locked up.'

He suddenly looked at her differently.

'What time is there a train for Paris?'

'In twenty minutes. After that there isn't another one until 12.39. Others pass through, but they don't stop at Orsenne.'

He was already halfway up the stairs. Without stopping to shave, he got dressed and a little later could be seen striding towards the station.

Her employer started thumping on the floor of her room, and Raymonde too went upstairs.

'Has he gone?' asked old Jeanne, who was still lying in her damp sheets.

'He's just left in a hurry.'

'Without saying anything?'

'No, madame.'

'Did he pay? Help me out of bed.'

'He didn't pay, madame, but he left his suitcase and all his things.'

'Oh!' said Jeanne, disappointed and possibly worried.

5. Maigret's Accomplice

Paris was wonderfully vast and empty. The cafés around Gare de Lyon smelled of beer and croissants dunked in coffee. Among other things, Maigret enjoyed a memorably cheerful quarter of an hour in a barber's shop on Boulevard de la Bastille, for no reason, simply because it was Paris on an August morning, and perhaps too because shortly he would be going to shake hands with his old friends.

'You're obviously just back from a holiday, you've really caught the sun.'

It was true. The previous day, probably, while he was running around Orsenne to check that Georges-Henry hadn't left the village.

It was funny how, from a distance, this affair lost its substance. But now, freshly shaven, the back of his neck bare, a little smudge of talcum powder behind his ears, Maigret clambered on to the running board of an omnibus and a few minutes later walked through the gates of the Police Judiciaire.

Here too, there was a holiday atmosphere and the air in the deserted corridors, where all the windows were wide open, had a smell he knew well. A lot of empty offices. In his or rather his former office, he found Lucas, who was dwarfed by the large space. Lucas leaped to his feet, as if ashamed to be caught out sitting in the chair of his former superior.

'You're in Paris, chief? . . . Have a seat.'

He immediately noticed Maigret's sunburn. That day, everyone would notice his sunburn and nine out of ten of them would not fail to remark with satisfaction:

'You've obviously come up from the country!'

As if he hadn't been living in the country for the last two years!

'Tell me, Lucas, do you remember Mimile?'

'Mimile from the circus?'

'That's right. I'd like to get hold of him today.'

'You sound as if you're on a case, chief.'

'A fool's errand, more like! Anyway . . . I'll tell you all about it another time. Can you track down Mimile?'

Lucas opened the door to the inspectors' office and spoke in a hushed voice. He must have been telling them the former chief was there and that he needed Mimile. During the half-hour that followed, nearly all of Maigret's former team contrived to pop into Lucas' office under some pretext or another, to come and shake hands with him.

'You've caught the sun, chief! You've obviously—'

'And another thing, Lucas. I could do it myself, but it's tiresome. I'd like the lowdown on the Amorelle and Campois firm of Quai Bourbon. The sand quarries of the Seine, the tug-boats and everything else.'

'I'll put Janvier on it, chief. Is it urgent?'

'I'd like to be done with it by midday.'

He mooched around HQ, dropped into the finance

division. They had heard of Amorelle and Campois, but they didn't have any inside information.

'A big outfit. They have a lot of subsidiaries. It's a robust concern and we haven't had any dealings with them.'

It was good to breathe the air of the place, to shake hands, to see the pleasure in every pair of eyes.

'So, how's your garden, chief? And what about the fishing?'

He went up to Criminal Records. Nothing on the Maliks. It was at the last moment, when he was on the point of leaving, that it occurred to him to search under the letter C.

Campois . . . Roger Campois . . . Hello, hello! There's a file on Campois: Roger Campois, son of Désiré Campois, industrialist. Blew his brains out in a hotel room on the Boulevard Saint-Michel.

He checked the dates, the addresses, the first names. Désiré Campois had indeed been the partner of old Amorelle, he was the man Maigret had glimpsed at Orsenne. He had been married to a certain Armande Tenissier, daughter of a civil engineering entrepreneur and now deceased, with whom he had had two children, a boy and a girl.

It was the boy, Roger, Désiré's son, who had committed suicide at the age of twenty-two.

For some months had been frequenting the gambling dens of the Latin Quarter and had recently lost heavily at the gaming tables.

As for the daughter, she had married and had borne a child, probably the young man he had seen with his grandfather at Orsenne.

Had she died too? What had become of her husband, a certain Lorigan? There was no mention in the file.

'Fancy a beer, Lucas?'

At the Brasserie Dauphine, of course, behind the Palais de Justice, where he had downed so many beers in his life. The air was pungent, like a fruit, with refreshing blasts punctuating the warm atmosphere. And it was a delightful sight to see a municipal street cleaner spraying wide bands of water on the tarmac.

'I wouldn't dream of questioning you, chief, but I confess that I'm wondering—'

'What I'm up to, eh? I'm wondering too. And it is highly likely that tonight I'll be getting myself into serious trouble. Look! Here comes Torrence!'

Fat Torrence, who had been tasked with locating Mimile, knew where to find him. He had already accomplished his mission.

'Unless he's changed his job in the last two days, chief, you'll find him working as an animal keeper at Luna Park. A beer!'

Then, Janvier, good old Janvier – how good they all were that day, and how good it was to be with them, how good it was to be working with the boys again! – Janvier too came and sat down at the table where an impressive pile of saucers had begun to accumulate.

'What exactly do you want to know about the Amorelle and Campois outfit, chief?'

'Everything . . .'

'Hold on . . .'

He took a scrap of paper out of his pocket.

'Old Campois, first of all. Arrived at the age of eighteen from his native Dauphiné. A wily and obstinate farmer. Initially employed by a building contractor in the Vaugirard neighbourhood, then by an architect, and then finally by a contractor in Villeneuve-Saint-Georges. That's where he met Amorelle.

'Amorelle, born in the Berry, married his boss's daughter. He and Campois became partners, and they both bought properties upstream from Paris, where they founded their first sand quarry company. That was forty-five years ago.'

Lucas and Torrence watched their former chief with an amused smile as he listened impassively. It was as though, while Janvier was speaking, Maigret's face had turned into that of the old days.

'I found all that out from an elderly employee who is vaguely related to a member of my wife's family. I knew him by sight and a few little drinks were enough to get him to talk.'

'Go on.'

'It's the same story as with all big companies. After a few years, Amorelle and Campois owned half a dozen sand quarries in the Haute Seine area. Then, instead of transporting their sand by barge, they bought boats. Well, tugs. Apparently it caused quite a stir at the time, because it was the ruin of the horse-drawn barges. There were demonstrations outside their offices on the Île Saint-Louis

. . . Because the offices, which were not so grand in those days, were already where they are today. Amorelle even received threatening letters. He stood his ground and it all blew over.

'Nowadays, it's a huge company. You can't imagine the size of a business like that, and it leaves me flabbergasted. They branched out into stone quarries. Then Amorelle and Campois bought shares in construction sites in Rouen where they had their tug-boats built. They now have majority shareholdings in at least ten businesses, shipping operations, quarries and shipbuilders, as well as civil engineering firms, and in a cement company.'

'What about the Maliks?'

'I'm coming to them. My man told me about them too. Apparently Malik number one—'

'What do you mean by number one?'

'The first to enter the company. Let me check my notes. Ernest Malik, from Moulins.'

'That's right.'

'He wasn't in the business at all, but was secretary to a high-up municipal councillor. That was how he met Amorelle and Campois. Because of the tenders. Bribes and all that! . . . And he married the eldest daughter. That was shortly after the suicide of the young Campois, who had been part of the firm.'

Maigret had withdrawn into himself and his eyes had narrowed to slits. Lucas and Torrence exchanged looks again, amused to see the chief as they had known him in his heyday, with his lips pursed around the stem of his pipe, his fat thumb stroking the bowl and that hunching of the shoulders.

'That's about all, chief . . . Once he'd joined the firm, Ernest Malik brought in his brother from some backwater. He was even less from that world. Some say that he was just a small insurance agent from the Lyon area. Even so, he married the second daughter and, since then, the Maliks have sat on all the boards of directors. Because the firm consists of a myriad of different companies that are interconnected. Apparently old Campois effectively has no authority. What's more, he was allegedly foolish enough to sell a huge number of shares when he believed they were at their peak.

'But, in opposition to the Maliks, there is still the old Amorelle widow, who can't stand them. And it is she who still has – at least it is thought she has – the majority shareholdings in the various companies. Company gossip has it that to infuriate her sons-in-law, she is capable of disinheriting them as far as the law allows.

'That's all I managed to dig up.'

A few more beers.

'Will you have lunch with me, Lucas?'

They had lunch together, like in the good old days. Then Maigret took an omnibus to Luna Park, where at first he was disappointed not to find Mimile in the menagerie.

'He's bound to be in one of the local cafés! You might find him in Le Cadran. Or perhaps at Léon's, unless he's at the tobacconist's on the corner.'

Mimile was at the tobacconist's and Maigret began by

buying him an aged *marc* brandy. He was a man of indeterminate age, with colourless hair, one of those men whom life has worn down like a coin to the point where they have no contours. You could never tell whether he was drunk or sober, for he always had the same hazy look, the same nonchalant air, from dawn till dusk.

'What can I do for you, boss?'

He had a criminal record at the Préfecture, quite a thick file. But he had calmed down years ago, and now did the occasional small favour for his former foe at Quai des Orfèvres.

'Can you leave Paris for twenty-four hours?'

'As long as I can find the Pole.'

'What Pole?'

'A fellow I know, but whose name is too complicated for me to remember. He was with Cirque Amar for a long time and he could take care of my animals. Let me telephone. A little drink first, eh boss?'

Two little drinks, three little drinks, a couple of brief calls from the telephone booth and finally Mimile announced:

'I'm your man!'

While Maigret explained what he wanted of him, Mimile had the dismayed look of a clown being hit repeatedly over the head with a stick, his rubbery lips repeating over and over again:

'Well I don't know, I really don't know ... It's only because it's you who's asking me to do it that I'm not reporting you to the police right away. Talk of a weird job, this is a weird job, all right.'

'Have you got it?'

'I've got it. I've completely got it.'

'Will you make sure you have everything you need?'

'And more! I know what I'm doing.'

As a precaution, Maigret drew him a little map of the place, checked the timetable and repeated his detailed instructions twice.

'Everything has to be ready by ten o'clock, I get it! You can count on me. As long as you're the one who takes the rap if there's trouble.'

They boarded the same train, shortly after four o'clock, pretending not to know each other, and Mimile, who had put an old bicycle belonging to the owner of the menagerie in the luggage compartment, got off one station before the Orsenne halt.

A few minutes later, Maigret calmly alighted, like an old regular, and lingered to chat to the crossing-keeper, who doubled as stationmaster.

He began by commenting that it was hotter in the country than in Paris, and it was true, for the heat in the valley was suffocating that day.

'Tell me, they must serve a reasonably decent white wine in that café, do they?'

The café was fifty metres from the station, and shortly the two men were sitting at a table with a bottle of white wine in front of them. Soon there was a series of little glasses in front of them too, that succeeded each other at an increasingly rapid rate.

An hour later, it was plain that the crossing-keeper would sleep well that night, and that was all that Maigret required of him.

As for him, he had made a point of spilling most of the alcohol that they had been served and he did not feel too sleepy as he ambled down to the river and a little later walked into the little garden of L'Ange.

Raymonde looked surprised to see him again so soon.

'What about Madame Jeanne?' he asked.

'She's still in her room. By the way, a letter arrived for you. It was delivered just after you left. Maybe the train hadn't arrived yet. If I hadn't been all alone, I'd have brought it to the station.'

With a black border, of course.

Monsieur,

I wish you to stop the investigation which I asked you to carry out in a moment of understandable depression, given my age and the recent shock I have suffered.

This may have led me to interpret certain tragic events in a way that is incompatible with the facts, and I now regret having disturbed you in your retirement.

Your presence at Orsenne only complicates an already pain-ful situation and I am taking the liberty of adding that the indiscretion with which you have set about the task I entrusted to you and the clumsiness you have exhibited so far prompt me to demand your immediate departure.

I hope you will understand and not insist on upsetting a family under a great deal of strain.

During my thoughtless visit to Meung-sur-Loire, I left a bundle of ten thousand francs on your table to cover your

initial expenses. You will find enclosed a cheque for the same
amount. Please consider this case over.

Yours sincerely,

Bernadette Amorelle

The note was indeed in her large, pointed handwriting, but it wasn't her style. Maigret gave a wry grimace and put the letter and the cheque in his pocket, convinced that the words he had just read were those of Ernest Malik rather than the elderly lady.

'I also have to tell you that Madame Jeanne asked me earlier when you were planning to leave.'

'Is she throwing me out?'

Plump Raymonde, whose curves were both sturdy and soft, blushed a deep red.

'That's not what I meant at all. It's just that she claims she's going to be ill for a while. When she has one of her attacks . . .'

He glanced covertly at the bottles that were the main reason for those attacks.

'And then?'

'The house is going to be sold any day now.'

'Once again!' said Maigret sardonically. 'And then what, dear Raymonde?'

'Don't you worry about me. I'd rather she'd told you herself. She says that it's not proper for me to be alone in the house with a man. She heard that the two of us ate together in the kitchen. She scolded me.'

'When does she want me to leave?'

'Tonight. Tomorrow morning at the latest.'

'And there are no other inns around here, are there?'

'There's one five kilometres away.'

'Well, Raymonde, we'll see about that tomorrow morning.'

'The thing is I've got no food this evening and I've been forbidden—'

'I'll eat up at the lock.'

Which he did. There was a little grocer's shop for the bargemen where drinks were served, as there are beside most locks. A group of boats was in the lock and the women, surrounded by their brood, were doing their shopping while the men came in for a quick drink.

All these people worked for Amorelle and Campois.

'Give me a bottle of white wine, a piece of sausage and half a pound of bread,' he ordered.

There was no restaurant. He sat down at the end of a table, and watched the water cascading over the lock gates. In the past, the barges used to make their way slowly along the banks, drawn by heavy horses which a little girl, often barefoot on the towpath, drove with a stick.

Those were the barges on which the horses used to sleep too that could still be seen on some canals but which, thanks to Amorelle and Campois' smoke-belching tug-boats and motorized barges, had disappeared from the Haute Seine.

The sausage was good, and the wine light, with a slightly acidic taste. The grocery shop smelled of cinnamon and oil. The upstream lock gates now open, the tug led its barges like chicks towards the top of the millrace and the lock-keeper came to have a drink at Maigret's table.

'I thought you had to leave tonight.'

'Who told you that?'

The lock-keeper looked sheepish.

'You know, if we listened to all the rumours we heard . . . !'

Malik was fighting back. He wasn't wasting any time. Had he come all the way to the lock himself?

From a distance, Maigret could see, amid the foliage, the roofs of the Campois' and the Amorelles' stately houses – that of the elderly Madame Amorelle and of her son-in-law, that of Ernest Malik, the most luxurious of all, that of Campois, halfway up the hill, almost rustic, although solidly bourgeois with its pink walls. On the other side of the water was the quaint, dilapidated little manor house of Monsieur Groux, who preferred to mortgage his properties rather than see his woods turned into quarries.

He wasn't far away, Monsieur Groux. You could see him, bareheaded in the sun, dressed as always in khaki, sitting in a green canoe moored between two poles and fishing with a rod and line.

There wasn't a breath of wind, no ripples on the water.

'You know about these things, don't you. Tell me, will there be a moon tonight?'

'That depends what time. It will rise just before midnight behind the wood you see upstream. It's in its first quarter.'

Maigret was fairly pleased with himself and yet he couldn't rid himself of a little knot of anxiety that had lodged in his chest and was growing instead of abating as the time passed.

A pang of nostalgia too. He had spent an hour at Quai des Orfèvres, with men he knew so well that they still called him chief, but who . . .

What had they said to each other after he had left? That he was missing the job, naturally! That life in his rural retreat wasn't as rosy as he would have them believe! That he had seized on the first opportunity to experience the thrills of the past again!

An amateur, in other words! He looked like an amateur.

'Another drop of white?'

The lock-keeper didn't say no. He had the habit of wiping his mouth with his sleeve after every sip.

'I am sure that young Malik – Georges-Henry – must have gone fishing lots of times with your son?'

'Oh yes, sir.'

'I expect he loved that, didn't he?'

'He loved the water, he loved the woods, he loved animals!'

'A good boy!'

'A good boy, yes. Not proud. If you could have seen the pair of them with the little young lady . . . They'd often go out together in the canoe. I'd offer to let them through the lock, even though we don't normally allow small boats through. But they were the ones who said no. They preferred to carry the boat to the other side of the lock. I'd see them going home at dusk.'

At dusk, or rather after dusk had fallen, Maigret himself had an unsavoury job to do. Then, everyone would know. They'd know whether he had got it wrong, if he was just an old dog who had deserved his retirement, or whether he was still good for something.

He paid and set off slowly along the riverbank, puffing away at his pipe. The wait was long, as if that evening the sun refused to go down. The shimmering water flowed slowly, silently, with only a barely perceptible murmur. The midges hovered dangerously close to the surface of the water, taunting the fish and making them jump.

He saw no one, neither the Malik brothers, nor their household servants. That evening everything was at a standstill. Shortly before ten o'clock, leaving behind him the light shining in Jeanne's room at L'Ange and in the kitchen where Raymonde sat, he made his way to the station, as he had done the previous night.

The little glasses of white wine had doubtless had their effect, because the crossing-keeper was not at his post outside his house. Maigret was able to walk past unseen and follow the track.

Behind the curtain of hazelnut trees, more or less at the spot where he had hidden the previous night, he found Mimile in position, a calm Mimile, legs apart, a cigarette that had gone out dangling from his lips, who seemed to be taking a breath of fresh air.

'No sign of him yet?'

'No.'

They stood waiting in silence. From time to time, they whispered a few words. As on the previous night, there was a window open in Bernadette Amorelle's apartment and they occasionally glimpsed the old lady moving around in the faint glow.

It was not until half past ten that a figure appeared in the Maliks' garden and things happened exactly as they had done the night before. The man was carrying a parcel and his dogs ran up to him then followed him to the door of the top kennel. He went inside, stayed a lot longer than the previous night and finally went back into the house, where a light went on at a first-floor window, which opened for a moment while the shutters were being closed.

The dogs roamed the gardens before settling down for the night, coming to sniff the air not far from the wall, doubtless sensing the presence of the two men.

'Shall I go, boss?' whispered Mimile.

One of the Great Danes snarled, as if about to growl, but the circusman had already thrown an object in its direction which landed on the ground with a soft thud.

'Unless they're better trained than I think,' muttered Mimile. 'But I'm not scared of that. These bourgeois folk don't know how to train dogs and even if they're given a well-trained animal, they soon spoil it.'

He was right. The two dogs prowled around the object, sniffing. Maigret, anxious, had let his pipe go out. Eventually one of the dogs gingerly picked up the meat in its mouth and shook it, while the other one, jealous, gave a menacing growl.

'There's enough for everyone!' sniggered Mimile, throwing a second piece. 'No need to fight, my beauties!'

The whole thing lasted barely five minutes. The pale hounds lurched about for a moment, then turned in circles, sick, and finally lay down on their sides. At that moment, Maigret was not proud of himself.

'It's done, boss. Shall we go?'

It was better to wait a little until it was completely dark and all the lights were out. Mimile was growing impatient.

'The moon will be up shortly and it'll be too late.'

Mimile had brought a rope which was already tied to the trunk of a young ash tree beside the track, close up against the wall.

'I'll go first.'

The wall was around three metres high, but it was in good condition, with no bulges.

'It will be harder to climb back over from here. Unless we find a ladder in their wretched garden. Oh look! There's a wheelbarrow down that little path. We can stand it up against the wall. That'll help.'

Mimile was excited, happy, like a man back in his element.

'If anyone had told me that I'd be doing this thing with you . . .'

They neared the former kennel or stable, which was a single-storey brick building with a concrete yard enclosed by a fence.

'No need for a torch,' whispered Mimile fiddling with the lock.

The door was open and they immediately caught a strong whiff of mouldy straw.

'Close the door! Well, it looks to me as if there's no one in here!'

Maigret switched on his torch and they saw nothing around them other than a broken old wooden stall, a mildewed harness hanging from a hook, a whip on the floor, and straw mixed with hay and dust.

'Down below,' said Maigret. 'There must be a hatch or an opening of some kind.'

They simply had to shift the straw to find a robust trap door with heavy hinges. The door was secured only with a bolt, which Maigret drew back slowly with a heavy heart.

'What are you waiting for?' hissed Mimile.

Nothing. And yet it had been years since he had felt that particular emotion.

'Do you want me to open it?'

No. He raised the trap door. Not a sound came from the cellar, and yet they both instantly had the feeling that there was a living creature down there.

The torch suddenly lit up the dark space below them, and the pale rays lighted on a face, a shape that leaped up.

'Stay calm,' said Maigret quietly.

He tried to track the shape with his torch as it darted from one wall to another like a hunted animal. He said mechanically:

'I am a friend.'

Mimile suggested:

'Shall I go down?'

And a voice from below said:

'Don't touch me!'

'Don't worry! No one's going to touch you.'

Maigret talked, talked as in a dream or rather as if trying to soothe a child who is having a nightmare. And the scene did indeed resemble a nightmare.

'Stay calm. Let's get you out of here.'

'What if I don't want to come out?'

The shrill, febrile voice of a mad child.

'Shall I go down?' Mimile offered again, keen to be done with things.

'Listen, Georges-Henry! I am a friend. I know everything.'

And suddenly it was as if he had spoken the magic words. The boy's agitation abruptly ceased. There was a few seconds' silence, then a changed voice asked warily:

'What do you know?'

'First of all we need to get out of here, young man. I promise you that you have nothing to fear.'

'Where's my father? What have you done with him?'

'Your father is in his bedroom, in bed, probably.'

'It's not true!'

His voice was full of animosity. They were lying to him. He was almost certain they were lying to him, as people had done all his life. This was the obsessive fear that his voice revealed to Maigret, who was beginning to lose patience.

'Your grandmother told me everything.'

'It's not true!'

'It was she who came to fetch me and who—'

And the boy, almost shouting:

'She doesn't know anything! I'm the only one who—'

'Hush! Trust me, Georges-Henry. Come. When you come out of here, we'll talk calmly.'

Would he let himself be cajoled? Otherwise Maigret would have to go down into the hole, use force, seize him bodily and overpower him, and he might fight back, scratch and bite like a panic-stricken young animal.

'Shall I go down?' repeated Mimile, who was growing restless and occasionally turned towards the door, afraid.

'Listen, Georges-Henry. I'm from the police.'

'This has nothing to do with the police! I hate the police! I hate the police!'

He broke off. An idea had just struck him and he continued in a different voice:

'Anyway, if you were the police you'd have—'

He shrieked:

'Leave me alone! Leave me alone! Go away! You're lying! You know you're lying! Go and tell my father—'

Just then, from over by the door which had opened noiselessly, a voice rang out:

'I'm sorry to disturb you, gentlemen.'

Maigret's torch lit up the shape of Ernest Malik, who was standing there, very calmly, a big gun in his hand.

'I believe, my poor Jules, that I would be within my rights to shoot you, along with your friend.'

From down below, they could hear the boy's teeth chattering.

6. Mimile and his Prisoner

Without betraying the least surprise, Maigret turned slowly towards the newcomer and appeared not to notice the gun pointing at him.

'Get the boy out of there,' he said in his most natural voice, like a man who, having tried to complete a task and failed, was asking another to try his hand.

'Now listen, Maigret—' Malik began.

'Not now. Not here. Later, I'll listen to anything you like.'

'Do you admit that you have put yourself in the wrong?'

'I'm telling you to take care of the child. You won't? Mimile, go down into the hole.'

Only then did Ernest Malik say sharply:

'You can come out, Georges-Henry.'

The boy did not move.

'Do you hear me? Come out! Your punishment has gone on long enough.'

Maigret shuddered. So that was what they would have him believe? That this was a punishment?

'That was hopeless, Ernest.'

And, leaning over the hole, he said in a calm, gentle voice:

'You can come now, Georges-Henry. You have nothing more to fear. Not from your father or from anyone else.'

Mimile held out his hand and helped the young man to hoist himself up through the trap door. Georges-Henry stood hunched, avoiding looking at his father, waiting for the chance to run away.

And that, Maigret had foreseen. For he had anticipated everything, even – and especially – Malik's bursting in on them. And Mimile had been given precise instructions, so now all he had to do was act on them.

The four of them could not stand there in the old kennel indefinitely, and Maigret was the first to walk towards the door, ignoring Malik, who stood barring his path.

'We'll be more comfortable talking inside the house,' he murmured.

'You insist on talking?'

Maigret shrugged. As he passed Mimile, he shot him a look that meant: 'Act with caution'.

For this was a delicate operation and one slip could ruin everything. They exited one by one and Georges-Henry emerged last, careful to keep a distance from his father. The four of them walked down the path and now it was Malik's turn to display a certain anxiety. The night was pitch black. The moon hadn't risen yet. Maigret had switched off his torch.

There was barely another hundred metres to go. What was the boy waiting for? Had Maigret got it wrong?

Now it was as if no one dared speak, no one wanted to take responsibility for what was about to happen.

Another sixty metres. In one minute, it would be too late and Maigret felt like giving Georges-Henry a nudge to bring him back down to earth.

Twenty metres . . . ten metres . . . Maigret would have to resign himself. What were the four of them going to do inside the house whose white façade loomed in front of them?

Five metres. Too late! Or rather it wasn't. Georges-Henry proved himself cannier than Maigret himself, for he had banked on one thing: once they reached the house, his father would have to go ahead to open the door.

At that exact moment he darted off and, a second later, the rustle of grasses and branches could be heard in the thicket. Mimile had been quick to spot the boy's move and set off in pursuit.

Malik barely lost a second, but it was a second too long. His reflex was to aim his gun at the circus-man's silhouette. He would have fired. But before he had time to squeeze the trigger, Maigret brought his fist down on his forearm and the gun clattered to the ground.

'And so we have it!' said Maigret with satisfaction.

He did not deign to pick up the weapon, which he kicked into the middle of the path. For his part, a sort of human pride prevented Ernest Malik from going to retrieve it. What would be the point?

The game being played now between the two of them could not in any way be affected by a gun.

For Maigret, it was quite an emotional moment. Precisely because he had anticipated it. The night was so still that they could hear, already some distance away, the footsteps of the two men running. Malik and he listened out. They could clearly hear that Mimile was close on the boy's heels.

They must have entered the neighbouring estate, still running, and from there they would probably head down to the towpath.

'And so we have it,' repeated Maigret as the sound faded until it was barely audible. 'Shall we go inside?'

Malik turned the key which he had inserted in the lock earlier and stood aside. Then he switched on the light and they saw his wife standing in a white bathrobe on the bend in the stairs.

She stared at the two of them, round-eyed in amazement and at a loss for words, until her husband snapped irritably:

'Go to bed!'

The two of them were in Malik's study and Maigret, standing, began to fill his pipe, darting smug little glances at his adversary. Meanwhile Malik paced up and down, his hands behind his back.

'Aren't you planning to lodge a complaint?' Maigret asked quietly. 'It's the perfect opportunity. Your two dogs poisoned. Climbing over the wall and trespassing. You could even claim there was a kidnap attempt . . . After sunset to boot . . . That would carry a sentence of hard labour. Go on, Ernest . . . The telephone is there, within reach. A call to the Corbeil gendarmerie and they'll have to arrest me.

'What's wrong? . . . What's stopping you?'

Using a familiar tone no longer bothered him now, quite the opposite, but it was not the chumminess Malik had used on their first meeting. It was the contemptuous familiarity that the former inspector used to employ with his 'customers'.

'Don't you want the whole world to know that you were keeping your son locked up in a cellar? . . . First of all, it's your right as a father. The right to punish. How many times, when I was little, was I threatened with being locked in the cellar!'

'Shut up, will you?'

Malik had planted himself in front of Maigret and was staring at him intently, trying to fathom what lay behind his words.

'What exactly do you know?'

'Finally! The question I've been waiting for.'

'What do you know?' asked Malik again, becoming impatient.

'And you, what are you afraid of me knowing?'

'I have already asked you not to poke your nose in my business.'

'And I refused.'

'For the second and last time, I'm telling you—'

But Maigret was already shaking his head.

'No . . . You see, that's impossible now.'

'You don't know anything.'

'In that case, what are you afraid of?'

'You won't find out anything.'

'So I'm not a bother to you, then.'

'As for the boy, he won't talk. I know you're relying on him.'

'Is that all you have to say to me, Ernest?'

'I'm asking you to think. I could have killed you earlier, and I'm beginning to wish I had.'

'You may well have been wrong not to. In a few moments, when I leave here, you'll still have a chance to shoot me in the back. It's true that now the boy is far away, and that there's someone with him. Come on! I'm ready for bed. So, no telephone? No complaint? No gendarmerie? Understood? Agreed?'

He headed for the door.

'Good night, Ernest.'

As he was about to disappear into the hall, he changed his mind and went back into the room, to say, with a solemn expression and a heavy gaze:

'You see, what I am going to discover is I suspect so ugly, so vile, that I'm loath to continue.'

He left without looking round, slamming the door hard behind him, and made his way to the gate, which was locked. The situation was absurd: here he was in the grounds of the house with no one to let him out.

The light was still on in the study, but Malik was not thinking about seeing his enemy off the premises.

Scale the back wall? Maigret did not think he was agile enough to do so alone. Find the path that would take him to the Amorelles' garden, where the gate might not be locked?

He shrugged and headed over to the gardeners' cottage, and tapped on the door.

'What is it?' came a sleepy voice from inside.

'A friend of Monsieur Malik's who needs someone to unlock the gate for him.'

He heard the old gardener moving around as he put on his trousers and hunted around for his clogs. The door opened a fraction.

'How come you are in the gardens? Where are the dogs?'

'I think they're asleep,' muttered Maigret. 'Unless they're dead.'

'What about Monsieur Malik?'

'He's in his study.'

'But he has the key to the gate.'

'Maybe. But he's so preoccupied that it didn't even occur to him.'

The gardener walked ahead of him, grumbling, turning round from time to time to dart an inquisitive look at this nocturnal visitor. When Maigret hastened his step, the man shuddered, as if he were expecting to be hit from behind.

'Thank you, my good man.'

He returned serenely to L'Ange. He had to throw pebbles at Raymonde's window to wake her and ask her to open the door.

'What time is it? I wasn't expecting you back tonight. Earlier I heard people running along the little path. Wasn't that you?'

He poured himself a drink and went to bed. At eight o'clock the next morning, freshly shaven and carrying his suitcase, he boarded the train for Paris. At half past nine, having drunk a coffee and eaten croissants in a little café, he walked into Quai des Orfèvres.

Lucas was conferring in his superior's office. Maigret sat down at his old desk, next to the open window, and an

Amorelle and Campois tug happened to be passing on the Seine, giving two loud siren blasts before disappearing under the Pont de la Cité.

At ten o'clock, Lucas came in, holding a sheaf of papers, which he set down on a corner of the desk.

'You're in town, chief? I thought you were back in Orsenne.'

'Has there been a telephone call for me this morning?'

'Not yet. Are you expecting one?'

'You need to inform the switchboard. Tell them to put the call directly through to me, or, if I'm not here, to take a message.'

He didn't want to appear anxious, but he smoked one pipe after another.

'Carry on with your work as if I weren't here.'

'Nothing exciting this morning. A stabbing in Rue Delambre.'

The daily routine. He knew it so well. He had removed his jacket, as in the old days when he was at home here. He wandered in and out of the various offices, shook hands, caught snatches of an interrogation or a telephone conversation.

'Don't mind me, boys.'

At half past eleven, he went down for a beer with Torrence.

'By the way, there's something I'd like you to find out for me. Still on the subject of Ernest Malik. I want to know if he's a gambler. Or if he was in the past, when he was young. It must be possible to find someone who knew him twenty or twenty-five years ago.'

'I will, chief.'

At a quarter to twelve, there was still nothing, and Maigret's shoulders grew more stooped, his gait more hesitant.

'I think I've been a complete idiot!' he even said to Lucas, who was dealing with routine business.

Each time the telephone rang in the office, he picked it up himself. At last, a few seconds before midday, someone was asking for Maigret.

'Maigret speaking . . . Where are you? . . . Where is he?'

'In Ivry, boss. I'll be quick, because I'm worried he'll take advantage. I don't know the name of the street. I didn't get a chance to see it. A little hotel. It's a three-storey building and the ground floor is painted brown. It's called A Ma Bourgogne. There's a gas works right opposite.'

'What's he doing?'

'I have no idea. I think he's sleeping. I'd better go.'

Maigret went and stood in front of a map of Paris and the suburbs.

'Do you know a gas works in Ivry, Lucas?'

'I think I get where it is, it's just past the station.'

A few minutes later, Maigret, sitting in an open-topped taxi, was heading towards the smoke of Ivry. He had to comb the streets for a while until he found a gas works and eventually spotted a seedy hotel whose ground floor was painted dark brown.

'Shall I wait for you?' asked the driver.

'I think that would be a good idea.'

Maigret walked into the restaurant area where workers, nearly all foreigners, were eating at the marble tables. A powerful smell of stew and cheap red wine assailed his throat. A sturdy girl in black and white wove among the tables, carrying an impossible number of small, grey ceramic dishes.

'Are you looking for the fellow who came down to telephone earlier? He said to tell you to go up to the third floor. You can go through here.'

A narrow corridor, with graffiti on the walls. The staircase was dark, lit only by a small window on the second floor. Once past it, Maigret caught sight of two feet and a pair of legs.

It was Mimile, sitting on the top stair, an unlit cigarette in his mouth.

'Give me a light first, boss. I didn't even stop to ask for matches when I went downstairs to telephone. I haven't been able to have a smoke since last night.'

There was a mixture of joy and mockery in his light-coloured eyes.

'Do you want me to shove over so you can sit down too?'

'Where is he?'

On the landing Maigret was able to make out four doors painted the same dreary brown as the façade. They bore the clumsily painted numbers 11, 12, 13 and 14.

'He's in number 12! I've got 13. It's funny, anyone would think they'd done it on purpose . . . Thirteen, unlucky for some!'

He inhaled the smoke avidly, stood up and stretched.

'If you'd like to come into my pad . . . but I warn you it stinks and the ceiling's low. While I was here on my own,

I thought it best to be out here and bar the way, you under-stand?'

'How did you manage to telephone?'

'Exactly . . . I'd been waiting for an opportunity all morning. 'Cause we've been here a while. Since six o'clock this morning.'

He opened the door of number 13, and Maigret glimpsed an iron bedstead painted black and an ugly reddish blan-ket, a straw-bottomed chair and a basin with no jug on a pedestal table. The third-floor rooms were under the eaves and, from the centre of the room, you had to stoop.

'Let's not stay here because he's as slippery as an eel. He's already tried to run off twice this morning. At one point I thought he might try and escape over the rooftops, but I realized that it's impossible.'

The gas works opposite, with its coal-blackened yards. Mimile had the tousled look of someone who hadn't slept and hadn't washed.

'We're actually better off on the stairs and it doesn't smell so bad. Here it stinks of sick flesh, don't you find? Like the smell of an old dressing.'

Georges-Henry was asleep, or was pretending to be, because when they pressed their ears to the door, they could not hear a sound from his room. The two men stayed on the staircase and Mimile explained, chain-smoking to catch up:

'First of all, how I managed to telephone you. I didn't want to leave my stakeout, as you police call it. But on the other hand, I had to contact you, as we'd agreed. At one point, at around nine o'clock, a woman came down, the one from number 14. I thought of asking her to give you a call, or to get a message to Quai des Orfèvres. Except that here, it might not be a very good idea to mention the police and I might have got myself thrown out.

'"Better wait for another opportunity, Mimile," I said to myself. "This is no time to get into a fight."

'When I saw the fellow from number 11 coming out of his room, I knew at once that he was a Pole. When it comes to Polish, I'm your man, I speak a bit of their language.

'I started to chat to him and he was very happy to hear his lingo. I told him some story about a chick. That she was in the room. That she wanted to ditch me. In short, he agreed to stand guard for the few minutes I needed to go downstairs and telephone.'

'Are you sure the kid is still in there?'

Mimile gave him a cheeky wink and took from his pocket a pair of pliers with which he gripped the tip of the key that was on the inside of the door but was protruding slightly from the keyhole.

He beckoned to Maigret to come over quietly and, with an extraordinarily gentle movement, he turned the key and opened the door a crack.

Maigret peered in and, in a room just like the one next door, whose window was open, he saw the young man stretched out fully clothed across the bed.

He was asleep, there was no doubt about it. He slept as boys of that age sleep, his features relaxed, his mouth half-open in a childlike pout. He had not taken his shoes off and one of his feet hung over the end of the bed.

Mimile shut the door again just as gently.

'Now let me tell you what happened. That was a brilliant idea of yours to have me take my bicycle. And an even more brilliant idea of mine to hide it near the level crossing.

'You remember how he raced off. A real rabbit. He zigzagged through the gardens and dived into the undergrowth hoping to shake me off.

'At one point, we went through a hedge, one after the other, and I still didn't manage to catch sight of him. It was the sound that told me that he was making for a house. Not exactly towards the house, but towards a sort of shed from which I saw him take out a bicycle.'

'His grandmother's house,' added Maigret. 'The bike must have been a woman's bike, the one belonging to his cousin Monita.'

'A woman's bike, yes. He jumped on to it, but he couldn't go fast along the garden paths, and I was still on his tail. I didn't dare talk to him yet, because I didn't know what was happening your end.'

'Malik wanted to shoot you.'

'I thought as much. It's funny, but I had a feeling. At one point I even stood still, for less than a second perhaps, as if I was waiting for the shot. Anyway, we were groping around in the dark again, and now he'd got off his bike and was pushing it. He passed it over another hedge. We found ourselves on a little path that ran down to the Seine and, there too, he couldn't go fast. On the towpath, it was different, and I lost a lot of ground, but I caught up with him on the way up to the station, because of the hill.

'He must have been quite confident, because he couldn't have guessed that I had my bike a bit further on.

'Poor kid! He was pedalling for all he was worth. He was certain he was going to throw me off, wasn't he?

'Well, he was wrong! I grab my bike in passing, I give it some oomph and, just when he's least expecting it, here I am riding alongside him as if nothing's happened.

'"Don't be afraid, kid," I say to him.

'I wanted to reassure him. He went crazy. He pedalled faster and faster, it made his breath all hot.

'"Don't be afraid, I'm telling you . . . You know Inspector Maigret, don't you? He doesn't want to hurt you, he wants to help you."

'From time to time, he turned towards me and yelled furiously:

'"Leave me alone!"

'Then, with a sob in his voice:

'"I still won't say anything."

'I felt sorry for him, I tell you. Some job you gave me. To say nothing of the fact that going down a hill, I can't remember where, on a main road, he swerves and ends up face down on the tarmac, and I literally heard the crack as his head hit the road.

'I get off my bike. I want to help him up. He was already back in the saddle, crazier, angrier than ever.

'"Stop, kid. You must have hurt yourself. There's no harm in us talking for a minute, is there? I'm on your side, I am."

'I'd been wondering for a while what he was up to, hunched over his handlebars, with one hand hidden from view. I should add that the moon had come up and it was fairly light.

'I ride up closer. I wasn't a metre away from him when he makes a movement. I duck. Luckily! That little rascal had just thrown a monkey wrench that he'd taken out of his saddle bag at my head. It missed my forehead by a whisker.

'Now he was even more frightened. He reckoned I was angry with him, that I'd get him back. And I carried on talking. It would be a laugh if I could repeat everything I said to him that night.

'"You realize that you won't get rid of me, don't you? Besides I'm under orders. Go where you like, you'll always find me behind you . . . I report to the inspector. Once he's there, this won't be my business any more."

'He must have taken the wrong road at a crossroads, because now we were heading away from Paris. After going through umpteen villages, all ghostly in the moonlight, we came out on Route d'Orléans. That's some distance from the Route de Fontainebleau!

'Eventually he was forced to slow down, but he refused to speak to me or even to look in my direction.

'Then it grew light and we were on the outskirts of Paris. I had another close shave, because he had the bright idea of diving into the little back streets to try and shake me off.

'He must have been worn out . . . I could see how pale he was, his eyelids were red. He only managed to stay on his bike through habit.

'"We'd do better to call it a night and get some kip, kid. You'll end up making yourself ill."

'And then, he spoke to me. He must have done it automatically, without realizing. Yes, I'm convinced he was so exhausted that he no longer knew what he was doing. Have you ever seen the finishing line of a cross-country race when the guy has to have someone holding him up while he's completely oblivious to all the excitement around him?

'"I don't have any money," he says to me.

'"That's not a problem, I do. We'll go wherever you like, but you need to rest."

'We were in this neighbourhood. I didn't think he'd take me at my word so quickly. He saw the word "hotel" over the door, which was open. There were some workers coming out.

'He got off the bike and he could barely stand up straight, he was so stiff. If the café had been open, I'd have bought him a drink, but I don't know if he'd have accepted it.

'He's proud, you know. He's a strange boy. I don't know what his plan is, but he's sticking to it, and it's not over yet.

'We shoved the two bikes under the stairs. If they haven't been stolen, they should still be there.

'He went up ahead of me. On the first floor, he didn't know what to do, because there didn't appear to be anyone around.

'"*Patron!*" I shouted.

'The owner turned out to be a woman. Stronger than a man, and difficult.

'"What do you want?"

'And she gave us a look that showed she was thinking dirty thoughts.

'"We want two rooms. Next to each other if possible."

'In the end she gave us two keys, rooms 12 and 13. That's all, boss. Now, if you don't mind staying here for a moment, I'd like to go and have a drink or two and maybe something to eat. I've been smelling food cooking since this morning.'

'Open the door for me,' said Maigret when Mimile came back up, reeking of alcohol.

'You want to wake him up?' protested Mimile, who had begun to consider the young man as his protégé. 'You'd do better to let him kip to his heart's content.'

Maigret gave a reassuring wave and went into the room without making a sound, tiptoeing over to the window and resting his elbows on the ledge. Men were loading the gas-works furnaces and the flames shot up bright yellow in the sunlight. He could imagine the sweat on the torsos of the workers stripped to the waist as they wiped their foreheads with their grimy arms.

It was a long wait. Maigret had plenty of time to think. From time to time, he turned towards his young companion, who was beginning to leave the realm of deep and peaceful sleep to enter into the more restless phase that precedes awakening. Sometimes his brow furrowed. His mouth opened wider, as if he were trying to say something. He was probably dreaming that he was speaking. He became fierce. He was saying 'no' with all the strength of his being.

Then his expression became more distraught and he appeared to be on the verge of tears. But he did not cry. He tossed and rolled over, making the sagging bed creak. He swatted a fly that had landed on his nose. His eyelids flickered, startled by the glare of the sunlight.

Finally his eyes were wide open, staring at the slanting ceiling in naive surprise. Then he gazed at the bulky form of Maigret, who stood with his back to the light.

Suddenly he was fully alert. He did not stir, but remained absolutely still, and a cold determination reminiscent of his father stole over his face and hardened his features.

'I still won't say anything,' he announced.

'I am not asking you to say anything,' replied Maigret with a hint of gruffness in his voice. 'And besides, what could you tell me?'

'Why was I followed? And what are you doing in my room? Where's my father?'

'He stayed back at home.'

'Are you sure?'

It was as if he did not dare budge, as if the slightest movement might put him in some unknown peril. He lay there on his back, his nerves on edge, his eyes wide.

'You have no right to follow me like this. I am free. I haven't done anything.'

'Would you rather I took you home to your father?'

Alarm in his grey eyes.

'That's what the police would do immediately if they caught you. You're a minor. You're just a child.'

Sitting up abruptly, the boy was overcome by despair.

'But I don't want to! . . . I don't want to! . . .' he howled.

Maigret heard Mimile moving around on the landing, no doubt thinking he was a bully.

'I want to be left alone. I want—'

Maigret caught the young man's panic-stricken glance in the direction of the window and understood. If he hadn't been blocking his path, Georges-Henry might have tried to throw himself out.

'Like your cousin?' he said slowly.

'Who told you that my cousin . . . ?'

'Listen, Georges-Henry.'

'No.'

'You have to listen to me. I know about the predicament you are in.'

'It's not true.'

'Do you want me to spell it out?'

'I forbid you. Do you understand?'

'Shh! . . . You can't go back to your father's house and you don't want to.'

'I'll never go back there.'

'What's more, you are in a frame of mind to do something stupid.'

'That's my business.'

'No. It's other people's business too.'

'Nobody cares about me.'

'The fact remains that you need someone to keep an eye on you for a few days.'

The young man sniggered ruefully.

'And that's what I have decided to do,' Maigret finished, calmly lighting his pipe. 'With or without your agreement . . . It's up to you which.'

'Where do you want to take me?'

It was already obvious that he was plotting his escape.

'I don't know yet. I admit that it's a tricky question, but, in any case, you can't stay in this dump.'

'It's no worse than a cellar.'

'Come, come!' This was a slight improvement since he was able to be ironic about his circumstances.

'First of all, we're going to have a nice lunch together. You're hungry. Of course you are.'

'It doesn't matter, I still won't eat.'

Heavens, he could be childish!

'Well I'm going to eat. I'm famished,' stated Maigret. 'And you will behave yourself. The friend you've already met and who followed you here is more agile than I am and he'll keep an eye on you. All right, Georges-Henry? You could do with a bath, but I don't see any chance of having one here. Wash your face.'

He obeyed sulkily. Maigret opened the door.

'Come in, Mimile. I suppose the taxi's still downstairs? The three of us are going for lunch somewhere, in a nice, quiet restaurant. Or rather the two of us, because you've already eaten.'

'I can eat again, don't worry.'

It sounded as though Georges-Henry had his feet back on the ground again since once they were downstairs he protested:

'What about the bikes?'

'We'll come back for them or send someone to pick them up.'

And, to the driver:

'Brasserie Dauphine.'

It was nearly three o'clock in the afternoon when they sat down to eat in the cool shade of the brasserie and an impressive selection of hors d'oeuvre dishes was placed in front of them.

7. Madame Maigret's Chick

'Hello! . . . Is that you, Madame Maigret? What? Where am I?'

That question reminded him of his days in the Police Judiciaire when he would go for four or five days without returning home, sometimes without being able to let his wife know where he was, and would finally telephone from the most unexpected places.

'In Paris, quite simply. And I need you. I'll give you half an hour to get dressed. I know . . . It's impossible . . . It doesn't matter . . . In half an hour, take Joseph's car . . . or rather Joseph will come and pick you up. What? Supposing it's not free? . . . Don't worry, I've already telephoned him. He'll drive you to Les Aubrais and the train will get in to Gare d'Orsay at six o'clock. Ten minutes later, a taxi will drop you off at Place des Vosges.'

This was the Maigrets' former Paris home, which they had kept. Without waiting for his wife to arrive, Maigret took Georges-Henry and Mimile to the apartment. The windows were protected with grey paper, there were dust covers and newspapers still on all the furniture, and flea powder on the rugs.

'I need a hand, boys.'

It could not be said that Georges-Henry had become more human during the meal. But although he hadn't uttered a word and had continued to look daggers at Maigret, at least he had eaten heartily.

'I still consider myself a prisoner,' he stated, once inside the apartment, 'and I warn you that I'll escape the minute I can. You have no right to keep me here.'

'That's right! Meanwhile, I need a hand over here, please!'

And Georges-Henry set to work with the others, folding the newspapers, removing the dust covers, and lastly pushing the electric vacuum cleaner around. They had finished and Maigret was pouring some Armagnac into three little glasses from the elegant set they hadn't taken to the country for fear of breaking it, when Madame Maigret arrived.

'Are you running a bath for me?' she asked in surprise at hearing the water pouring into the bathtub.

'No, darling. It's for this young man, a charming boy who's going to be staying here with you. His name is Georges-Henry. He has promised to run away at the first opportunity, but I'm relying on Mimile – let me introduce him, by the way – and on you to stop him from leaving. Do you think you've digested your lunch, Georges-Henry? Then go and have a bath.'

'Are you leaving? . . . Will you be back for dinner? . . . You don't know, as usual! And there's nothing to eat here.'

'You've got all the time in the world to go shopping while Mimile keeps an eye on the boy.'

He whispered a few things to her and she looked at the bathroom door with a sudden tenderness.

'All right! I'll try. How old is he? Seventeen?'

Half an hour later, Maigret found himself in the family atmosphere of the Police Judiciaire, asking for Torrence.

'He's back, chief. He should be in his office, unless he's gone down for a beer. I left a message for you on your old desk.'

It was about a telephone call that had come in at around three o'clock:

Please tell Detective Chief Inspector Maigret that last Monday Bernadette Amorelle had her lawyer come to draw up her will. He is Maître Ballu, who probably lives in Paris.

The switchboard operator couldn't say exactly where the telephone call had originated. She had simply heard an operator saying:

'Hello! Corbeil! I'm putting you through to Paris.'

It probably came from Orsenne or nearby.

'It was a woman's voice. I may be wrong, but I had the impression that it was someone who was not in the habit of making telephone calls.'

'Ask Corbeil where the telephone call originated.'

He went into the office of Torrence, who was busy writing a report.

'I made inquiries as you requested, chief. I contacted a dozen or so clubs, but I only found traces of Ernest Malik at two of them, the Haussmann and the Sporting. Malik still goes to them occasionally, but much less regularly than in the past. Apparently he's a poker ace. He never goes near the baccarat table. Poker and écarté. He rarely loses! At the Sporting, I was lucky enough to come across an old gambling inspector I used to know thirty years ago.

'When he was still a student, Malik was one of the best poker players in the Latin Quarter. The old inspector, who was a waiter at La Source at that time, claims that he earned his living at cards.

'He set himself a figure which he never exceeded. As soon as he'd won that amount, he had the self-control to withdraw from the game, which made him unpopular with his partners.'

'Have you ever come across a lawyer called Ballu?'

'That name rings a bell. Hold on!'

Torrence flicked through a directory.

'Batin . . . Babert . . . Bailly . . . Ballu . . . 75, Quai Voltaire. It's just across the road!'

Strangely, this lawyer business troubled Maigret. He didn't like it when a new lead suddenly emerged and disrupted his investigation, and he was tempted to ignore this one.

The switchboard operator informed him that the call had come from the post office in Seine-Port, five kilometres from Orsenne. The postmistress, questioned over the telephone, answered that the caller had been a woman aged around twenty-five to thirty, and that was all she could say.

'I didn't get a chance to look at her, because it was the time when they come to collect the mail bags. What? She looked like a worker . . . Yes! A maid perhaps.'

Wasn't it just like Malik to get one of his servants to call?

Maigret gave his name on arrival at Maître Ballu's practice. His office was closed, but he agreed to see Maigret.

He was extremely elderly, almost as old as Bernadette Amorelle herself. His lips were nicotine-stained, and he spoke in a reedy, cracked voice, then held a tortoiseshell ear trumpet towards his visitor.

'Amorelle! Yes, I can hear you. She is indeed an old friend! We go back . . . Wait . . . It was before the 1900 World's Fair that her husband came to see me about a land matter. A strange man! I remember asking him whether he was a relative of the Geneva Amorelles, an old Protestant family who . . .'

He declared that he had indeed been to Orsenne the Monday of the previous week. And yes, Bernadette Amorelle has asked him to draw up a new will. He could not say anything about the contents of the will itself, of course. It was there, in his antiquated safe.

Whether there had been other, previous wills? Perhaps ten, perhaps more? Yes, his old friend was in the habit of making wills, an innocent habit, wouldn't you agree?

Was Monita Malik named in this new document? The lawyer was sorry, but he couldn't say anything on that subject. Professional confidentiality!

'She's as fit as a fiddle! I'm certain that this is not her last will and that I will once again have the pleasure of going to visit her.'

So Monita had died twenty-four hours after the lawyer's visit to Orsenne. Were the two events connected?

Why on earth had someone taken the trouble to throw this new information in Maigret's face, as it were?

He walked along the Seine. He was on his way home to have dinner with his wife, Georges-Henry and Mimile.

From the Pont de la Cité, he saw a tug-boat chugging up the Seine with its five or six barges. An Amorelle and Campois tug-boat. Just then, a spanking new big yellow taxi, the latest model, drove past, and these two minor details probably influenced his decision.

He didn't stop to think. He raised his arm. The taxi drew up by the kerb.

'Have you got enough petrol for a long drive?'

Maybe if the car's fuel tank hadn't been full . . .

'Route de Fontainebleau. After Corbeil, I'll direct you.'

He hadn't had dinner, but he had eaten a late lunch. He asked the driver to stop at a tobacconist's so he could buy a packet of shag and some matches.

It was a mild evening and the taxi had its roof down. He had sat next to the driver, perhaps with the intention of starting a conversation. But he barely opened his mouth.

'Turn left here.'

'Are you going to Orsenne?'

'Do you know it?'

'Years ago I sometimes drove guests to L'Ange.'

'We're going further. Continue along the towpath. It's not this house, or the next one. Keep going.'

They had to take a narrow track on the right to reach the Campois house, which could not be seen from the outside for it was completely enclosed by walls and, instead of an iron gate, there was a solid double door, painted light green.

'Wait for me!'

'I've got plenty of time! I'd just had dinner when you flagged me down.'

Maigret pulled the bell cord and from the garden came

a pleasant peal like that of a presbytery. There was an ancient boundary stone either side of the entrance and a little door set in one of the big wooden panels.

'Doesn't look as if anyone's going to answer,' commented the driver.

It was not late – just after eight o'clock in the evening. Maigret rang again and this time footsteps could be heard crunching the gravel; an elderly cook in a blue apron turned a heavy key in the lock, opened the little door a crack and eyed Maigret warily.

'What do you want?'

He glimpsed a densely planted secluded garden, full of simple flowers and unexpected nooks and crannies overgrown by weeds.

'I'd like to speak to Monsieur Campois.'

'He's left.'

She was already about to close the door, but he had stepped forwards to stop her.

'Can you tell me where I might find him?'

Did she know who he was from having seen him prowling around Orsenne?

'You won't be able to find him. Monsieur Campois has gone abroad.'

'For long?'

'For at least six weeks.'

'Forgive me for insisting, but it is about a very important matter. May I at least write to him?'

'You can write to him if you like, but I doubt he'll receive your letters before his return. Monsieur is on a cruise to Norway aboard the *Stella-Polaris*.'

Just then, Maigret heard, in the garden behind the house, the sound of an engine spluttering to life.

'Are you sure he has already left?'

'I'm telling you—'

'What about his grandson?'

'He has taken Monsieur Jean with him.'

Maigret had a struggle to push the door open because the cook was trying to close it forcefully.

'What's wrong with you? Where are your manners?'

'What's wrong with me is that Monsieur Campois hasn't left yet.'

'That's his business. He doesn't want to see anyone.'

'But he will see me.'

'Will you get out of here, you rude man!'

Rid of the cook, who was meticulously locking the door behind him, Maigret crossed the garden and came upon a modest pink house with climbing roses invading the green-shuttered windows.

As he looked up, his gaze lighted on an open window and at this window stood a man who was watching him with a sort of terror.

It was Monsieur Campois, the late Amorelle's partner.

There were trunks in the wide hall, where the atmosphere was pleasantly cool and smelled of ripening fruit. The elderly cook joined him:

'Well, if Monsieur said it's all right for you to come in . . .' she grumbled.

And she reluctantly showed him into a sitting room that resembled a parlour, with, in one corner, by a window with half-closed shutters, one of those old black desks that evoked trading companies of the past, with their green filing cabinets, the clerks perched on tall chairs, a ring of leather under their buttocks and a peaked cap pulled down over their eyes.

'Just wait here! Too bad if he misses his ship.'

The walls were covered in faded wallpaper and, against this wallpaper, photographs stood out in their black or gilt frames. There was the inevitable wedding photo, a Campois already plump, his hair in a crew cut, and, leaning against his shoulder, the face of a woman with full lips and a gentle, sheeplike gaze.

Immediately to the right, a young man aged around twenty, his face more elongated than that of his parents, his eyes softer, he too looking shy and timid. And, beneath that frame, a black crepe bow.

Maigret was walking over to a piano covered in photographs when the door opened. Campois stood in the doorway and Maigret thought he looked smaller and older than when he had first set eyes on him.

He was already a very old man, despite his sturdy farmer's build.

'I know who you are,' he said straight off. 'I couldn't refuse to see you, but I have nothing to say to you. I'm leaving in a moment for a long trip.'

'Where are you sailing from, Monsieur Campois?'

'From Le Havre, which is where the cruise leaves from.'

'You're probably catching the 10.22 train from Paris? You'll make it.'

'Please excuse me, but I haven't finished packing. Nor

have I had dinner yet. I repeat that I have absolutely nothing to say to you.'

What was he afraid of? Because it was clear that he was afraid of something, that was clear. He was dressed in black, with a black detachable tie, and the paleness of his complexion contrasted sharply with the darkness of the room. He had left the door open, as if to signal that this conversation would have to be brief, and he did not invite his visitor to sit down.

'Have you been on many cruises of this kind?'

'It's . . .'

Was he about to lie? He certainly wanted to. He gave the impression that he needed someone beside him to feed him his lines. His old honesty prevailed. He didn't know how to lie. He admitted:

'It's the first time.'

'And you are seventy-five years old?'

'Seventy-seven!'

Go for it! It was best to stake his all. The poor man wasn't capable of defending himself for long and his frightened gaze showed that he was beaten from the start, and was perhaps already resigned to the fact.

'I am certain, Monsieur Campois, that up until three days ago, you had no idea you would be going on this voyage. I would even wager that you're a little afraid! The Norwegian fjords, at your age!'

He stammered, as if giving a rehearsed answer:

'I've always wanted to visit Norway.'

'But you weren't planning on going there this month! Someone planned it for you, didn't they?'

'I don't know what you mean. My grandson and I—'

'Your grandson must have been as surprised as you. For the moment it matters little who arranged this cruise for you. By the way, do you know where the tickets were purchased?'

Campois had no idea, as his alarmed expression showed. He had been given a part to play. He was playing it to the best of his ability, but there were events that had not been foreseen, including Maigret's sudden intrusion, and the poor man didn't know which way to turn.

'Listen, inspector, I repeat that I have nothing to say to you. I am in my own home. I'm leaving shortly for a cruise. Acknowledge that I have the right to ask you to leave me alone.'

'I came to talk to you about your son.'

As he had foreseen, old Campois became perturbed, turned ashen and shot an anguished look at the portrait.

'I have nothing to say to you,' he repeated, clinging to those words that no longer meant anything.

Maigret listened out, having heard a faint noise in the corridor. Campois must have heard it too, and he made for the door:

'Leave us, Eugénie. The luggage can be put in the car. I'm coming straight away.'

This time, he closed the door and went and sat mechanically in his place, at the desk which must have followed him throughout his long career. Maigret sat down opposite him without being invited to do so.

'I've thought long and hard about your son's death, Monsieur Campois.'

'Why have you come to talk to me about that?'

'You know very well. Last week, a young girl whom you know died in the same circumstances. Earlier, I left a young man who very nearly came to the same end. And it's your fault, isn't it?'

He protested emphatically:

'My fault?'

'Yes, Monsieur Campois! And you know it. You may not want to admit it, but deep down—'

'You have no right to come to my house and say such dreadful things to me. I've been an honest man all my life.'

But Maigret did not allow him the time to wallow in protestations.

'Where did Ernest Malik meet your son?'

The old man drew his hand across his forehead.

'I don't know.'

'Were you already living in Orsenne?'

'No! In those days I lived in Paris, on the Île Saint-Louis. We had a big apartment above our offices, which weren't as big as they are nowadays.'

'Did your son work in those offices?'

'Yes. He had just obtained his law degree.'

'Did the Amorelles already have their house in Orsenne?'

'They arrived here first, yes. Bernadette was a very busy woman. She loved to entertain. She was always surrounded by young people. On Sundays, she would invite lots of friends to the country. My son used to come too.'

'Was he in love with the eldest Amorelle daughter?'

'They were engaged.'

'And did Mademoiselle Laurence love him?'

'I don't know. I imagine so. Why are you asking me that? After all these years . . .'

He would have liked to release himself from this sort of spell that Maigret had cast over him. Twilight was gathering in the room where the portraits stared down at them with their dead eyes. Mechanically, the old man had picked up a meerschaum pipe with a long cherrywood stem, which he didn't think of filling with tobacco.

'How old was Mademoiselle Laurence at the time?'

'I can't remember. I'll have to count. Wait . . .'

He muttered dates half-heartedly, as if saying a rosary. His brow furrowed. Perhaps he still hoped that someone would come and save him?

'She must have been seventeen.'

'So her younger sister, Mademoiselle Aimée, was barely fifteen?'

'That must be right, yes. I've forgotten.'

'And your son met Ernest Malik, who, unless I'm mistaken, was at the time private secretary to a municipal councillor. It was through that councillor that he himself met the Amorelles. He was a brilliant young man.'

'Maybe . . .'

'He became friends with your son and, under his influence, your son changed?'

'He was a very good boy, a very gentle boy,' protested the father.

'Who started gambling and got into debt—'

'I didn't know.'

'Bigger and bigger debts, more and more blatant. Things got so bad that he ended up having to live by his wits.'

'It would have been better if he'd told me everything.'

'Are you sure you would have understood?'

The old man hung his head and admitted:

'At that time, I might—'

'You might not have understood, you might have thrown him out. If he had told you, for example, that he'd taken the money from your partner's coffers, or that he'd falsified the accounts, or—'

'Be quiet!'

'He preferred to die. Perhaps because he was advised to kill himself? Perhaps . . .'

Campois wiped both hands over his anguished face.

'But why come and speak to me of all this today? What are you hoping for? What are you trying to achieve?'

'Admit, Monsieur Campois, that at that time, you thought what I am thinking today.'

'I don't know what you are thinking . . . I don't want to know!'

'Even if at the time of your son's death you weren't suspicious straight away, you must have started to wonder when Malik married Mademoiselle Amorelle a few months later. You follow me, don't you?'

'I couldn't do anything.'

'And you attended the wedding!'

'I had to. I was Amorelle's friend, his partner. He worshipped Ernest Malik, who in his eyes could do no wrong.'

'So you kept quiet.'

'I had a daughter who was still unmarried and I needed to find her a husband.'

Maigret rose, burly, threatening, and gave the crushed old man a look full of intense anger.

'And, for years and years, you have . . .'

His voice, which had risen, softened again as he watched the face of the elderly man, whose eyes filled with tears.

'But for goodness' sake,' Maigret went on with a sort of dread, 'you knew all along that it was Malik who killed your son.

'Yet you said nothing!

'Yet you carried on shaking hands with him!

'Yet you bought this house close to his!

'And still today, you're willing to do as he tells you!'

'What choice did I have?'

'Because he drove you to the brink of poverty. Because, through God-knows-what cunning schemes, he managed to divest you of most of your shares. Because now you are merely a name in the Amorelle and Campois concern. Because—'

And his fist came down on the desk.

'But dammit! Don't you realize you are a coward, that it's because of you that Monita is dead like your son and that a boy, Georges-Henry, nearly followed suit?'

'I have my daughter and my grandson. I am old!'

'You weren't old when your son died. But you were already so obsessed with money that you weren't even capable of standing up to a Malik.'

It was almost dark now in the long room where it hadn't occurred to either of the two men to switch on the light.

Visibly terrified, the old man asked in a dull voice:

'What are you going to do?'

'What about you?'

Campois' shoulders slumped.

'Are you still planning to go on this cruise that doesn't appeal to you at all? You can't see, can you, that you're being sent away in haste, the way the weak are sent away in a crisis? When was this cruise decided on?'

'Malik came to see me yesterday morning. I didn't want to, but in the end I gave in.'

'What excuse did he give?'

'That you were poking around in our business affairs and trying to cause trouble for us. That it would be better if I weren't around.'

'Did you believe him?'

The old man did not reply, and continued after a while in a weary voice:

'He's already been here three times today. He caused havoc to speed up my departure. Half an hour before you arrived, he telephoned me again to remind me that it was time to leave.'

'Are you still intent on going?'

'I think it's best, given what is probably going to happen. But I could stay in Le Havre. It depends on my grandson. He used to spend a lot of time with Monita. I think he cherished hopes about her. He was very upset by her death.'

The old man suddenly sprang up and rushed towards the old-fashioned telephone on the wall. It had given a strident ring, calling him to order.

'Hello! Yes . . . The luggage is in the car. I'm leaving in five minutes . . . Yes . . . Yes . . . No . . . No . . . It wasn't for me . . . Probably . . .'

He hung up and darted a slightly sheepish look at Maigret.

'It's him. I'd better leave.'

'What did he ask you?'

'If anyone had been to see me. He saw a taxi go past. I told him—'

'I heard.'

'Can I leave?'

What was the point of stopping him? He had worked hard in the past. He had succeeded by the sweat of his brow. He had achieved an enviable position.

And, for fear of losing his money, for fear of the poverty he had known as a child, he had been scared out of his wits. And now he had reached the end of his life, he was still scared.

'Eugénie! Is the luggage in the car?'

'But you haven't had dinner!'

'I'll have something to eat on the way. Where is Jean?'

'By the car.'

'Goodbye, inspector. Don't say that you've seen me. If you carry on down the little path and turn left, you'll see a stone cross, and you'll come out on to the main road three kilometres from here. There's a tunnel under the railway track.'

Maigret slowly crossed the garden that lay bathed in tranquillity, the cook following him stealthily. The taxi-driver was sitting on the grass bordering the path playing with the wild flowers. Before getting back into the car, he put one behind his ear, the way mischievous boys wedge a cigarette.

'Do we turn round?'

'Straight on,' grunted Maigret, lighting his pipe. 'Then left when you see a cross.'

It was not long before they heard in the darkness the engine of another car going in the opposite direction, that of old Campois heading for safety.

8. The Skeleton in the Cupboard

To stoke his ill humour, he asked the taxi to stop at a poorly lit café in Corbeil and ordered two glasses of *marc*, one for the driver and the other for himself.

The bitter taste of the brandy made his throat constrict, and he said to himself that *marc* had been a feature of this investigation. Why? Pure chance. It was probably the drink he least liked. Besides, there had also been old Jeanne's disgusting Kummel, and that memory, that tête-à-tête with the bloated old alcoholic, still made him feel nauseous.

Yet she had once been beautiful. He now knew that she had loved Malik, who had used her the way he used everyone and everything. And now it was a curious mixture of love and hatred, of bitterness and animal devotion that she nursed for this man, who only needed to appear and snap his fingers for her to do his bidding.

There are people like that in the world. There are others, like these two customers in the little bar, the only two customers at this late hour, a fat man, who was a pork butcher, and a shrewd, thin character who likes pontificating, proud of being a clerical worker, maybe at the town hall, both of them playing draughts at ten o'clock at night beside a huge stove pipe against which the pork butcher leaned from time to time.

The pork butcher was self-confident because he had

money and it didn't matter if he lost the round. The skinny man thought that life was unfair because an educated man with a degree should have a more comfortable existence than a butcherer of pigs.

'Another *marc* . . . sorry, two *marcs!*'

Campois and his grandson were on their way to Gare Saint-Lazare. He too must be all churned up. He was probably mulling Maigret's harsh words in his mind and reliving old memories.

He was heading for Le Havre. He had nearly set sail for the Norwegian fjords, against his wishes, dispatched there like a parcel, because Malik . . . And he was already a very old man. It is tough telling elderly people like him home truths, as Maigret had just done.

They were back in the car. Maigret sat in his corner, glum and scowling.

Bernadette Amorelle was even older. And what he didn't know, what he couldn't know, because he wasn't God Almighty, was that she had seen old Campois drive past in his car laden with trunks.

She too had understood. Perhaps she was cleverer than Maigret? There are women, old women especially, who have a real gift of second sight.

If Maigret had been there, beside the railway track, as he had been on the two previous nights, he would have seen her three windows open, with the lights on, and in that rosy glow, the old lady calling her maid.

'He made old Campois leave, Mathilde.'

He wouldn't have heard, but he would have seen the two women have a long conversation, each as peevish as the other, then he would have seen Mathilde vanish, Madame Amorelle pacing up and down her room, and finally her daughter Aimée, Charles Malik's wife, come in looking guilty.

The drama was unfolding. It had been brewing for over twenty years. For the past few days, since Monita's death, it had been threatening to explode any minute.

'Stop here!'

Bang in the middle of the Pont d'Austerlitz. He didn't feel like going straight back home. The Seine was black. There were little lights on the sleeping barges, shadows roaming the banks.

His hands in his pockets, Maigret smoked as he walked slowly through the empty streets where the lamps made strings of lights.

At Place de la Bastille, at the corner of Rue de la Roquette, the lights were brighter, lurid, with that pallid glare typical of poor neighbourhoods – like those fairground stalls where you can win packets of sugar or bottles of sparkling wine – lights to lure the people out of their dark, narrow, suffocating streets.

He too walked towards those lights, towards the too vast and too empty café where an accordion was playing and where a few men and a few women were drinking and waiting for who-knows-what.

He knew them. He had spent so many years dealing with people's everyday doings that he knew them all – even people like Malik, who think they are more powerful or cleverer than the rest.

With that type, there's a difficult moment to get through, when, despite yourself, you allow yourself to be impressed by their beautiful house, their car, their servants and their airs.

You have to see them like the others, to see them naked . . .

Now, it was Ernest Malik who was frightened, as frightened as a small-time pimp from Rue de la Roquette who has been carted off in the meat wagon at two o'clock in the morning.

Maigret did not see the two women in Bernadette's bedroom acting out a heart-breaking scene. He did not see Aimée drop to her knees on the rug and drag herself kneeling over to her mother's feet.

This no longer mattered. Every family has a skeleton in the cupboard.

Two beautiful houses, down there by the river, on an attractive bend where the Seine widened, two beautiful houses surrounded by greenery against the gentle hills, the sort of houses that make people sigh longingly as they gaze at them from trains.

Those living in them must be so happy!

And long lives, like that of Campois, who had worked hard, and who was now worn out and being shunted aside.

And that of Bernadette Amorelle, who had dispensed so much frantic energy.

He walked furiously. Place des Vosges was deserted. There was a light at his windows. He rang the bell and growled his name as he passed the concierge's lodge. His wife, who recognized his step, came and opened the door.

'Shh! He's asleep. He's only just dropped off.'

So what? Wasn't he going to wake him up, grab him by the shoulders and shake him?

'Come on, young man, this is no time to make a fuss.'

Let's put an end once and for all to this skeleton in the cupboard, to this vile business, which, from start to finish, was all a filthy matter of money.

For that is all there was behind those beautiful houses with their immaculate gardens: money!

'You look grumpy. Have you had dinner?'

'Yes . . . No.'

Actually, he hadn't had dinner and he ate while Mimile stood at the window, smoking cigarettes. When Maigret started walking towards the guest room, where Georges-Henry was sleeping, Madame Maigret protested:

'You shouldn't wake him.'

He shrugged. A few hours more or less . . . Let him sleep! Not to mention that he was tired too.

He could not guess that Bernadette Amorelle had stolen out of her house alone, in the middle of the night, and that her younger daughter, Aimée, her eyes crazed, tried in vain to telephone, while Charles, behind her, kept repeating:

'What on earth's wrong with you? What did your mother say to you?'

Maigret did not wake up until eight o'clock the next morning.

'He's still asleep,' his wife announced.

Maigret shaved, dressed and had breakfast on a corner of the table, then filled his first pipe. When he went into the young man's room, Georges-Henry began to stir.

'Get up,' he said in that calm, slightly weary voice that he used when he was determined to put an end to something.

It took him a few moments to realize why the boy wouldn't get out of bed. He was naked under the sheets and didn't dare show himself.

'Stay in bed if you like. You can get dressed later. How did you find out what your father had done? It was Monita who told you, wasn't it?'

Georges-Henry stared at him in genuine horror.

'You can talk, now that I know—'

'What do you know? Who told you?'

'Old Campois knew too.'

'Are you sure? He couldn't have. If he'd known—'

'That your father killed his son? Only he didn't kill him with a knife or a bullet. And those murders—'

'What else have you been told? What have you done?'

'Well, there are so many vile doings in this business that one more or one less . . .'

He felt sick. That often happened to him when he reached the end of an investigation, perhaps because of the strain, perhaps because, when a man is stripped naked, what you find tends to be ugly and depressing.

A pleasant smell of coffee filled the apartment. You could hear the birds and the fountains of Place des Vosges. People were going off to work in the cool, gentle morning sunlight.

In front of him, a pale kid who had pulled the blankets up to his chin and was gazing steadfastly at him.

What could Maigret do for him, for the others? Nothing!

You don't arrest a Malik. The law didn't deal with those crimes. There would only be one solution . . .

It is funny that he thought of it just before the telephone call. He was standing there, puffing on his pipe, ill-at-ease with this boy who did not know what to do, and for a second he had a vision of Ernest Malik with someone handing him a pistol, calmly giving him the order:

'Shoot!'

But he wouldn't shoot! He would never agree to kill himself! He would need help.

The telephone rang insistently. Madame Maigret answered then knocked at the door.

'It's for you, Maigret.'

He went into the dining room and grabbed the receiver.

'Hello . . .'

'Is that you, chief? Lucas here. When I arrived in my office I found an urgent message for you from Orsenne, yes . . . Last night, Madame Amorelle . . .'

Probably no one would have believed him if he had claimed that, from that moment, he knew. And yet it was true.

She had followed more or less the same reasoning as him, of course! She had reached the same conclusions, almost at the same time. Except that unlike him, she had seen things through to the bitter end.

And, since she knew that a Malik wouldn't shoot, she had calmly pulled the trigger.

' . . . Madame Amorelle killed Ernest Malik with a pistol shot. At his home, yes . . . in his study. He was in his pyjamas and dressing gown. The gendarmerie telephoned here at dawn asking us to inform you, because she's asking to see you.'

'I'll go,' he said.

He went back into the bedroom where the young man had put on his trousers, his bare chest painfully thin.

'Your father is dead,' said Maigret, averting his gaze.

A silence. He turned round. Georges-Henry was not crying, but stood stock still, looking at him.

'Did he kill himself?'

So they weren't two but three of them to have thought of the same solution. Who knows whether the kid hadn't been tempted, at one point, to pick up the gun?

There was still a trace of incredulity in his voice as he asked again:

'Did he kill himself?'

'No. It was your grandmother.'

'Who told her?'

He was biting his lips.

'Who told her what?'

'What you know . . . Campois?'

'No, son. That's not what you were thinking of.'

And the boy turned red, proving Maigret right.

'There's something else, isn't there? It's not because in the past your father drove the Campois boy to commit suicide that Bernadette Amorelle killed him.'

He paced up and down. He could have pressed the matter. He would have defeated an opponent who was not an equal match for him.

'Stay here,' he said at last.

He went to fetch his hat from the dining room.

'Keep an eye on him,' he shouted to his wife and Mimile, who was now having his breakfast.

It was a glorious day, the air so delicious in its morning freshness that you felt like biting into it, like a fruit.

'Taxi . . . Route de Fontainebleau. I'll direct you.'

There were three or four cars on the towpath, those of the public prosecutor, no doubt. A few curious onlookers in front of the gate, where an indifferent gendarme stood guard. He greeted Maigret, who walked down the drive and was soon mounting the steps.

The detective chief inspector from the Melun Flying Squad was already there, his hat on his head, a cigar in his mouth.

'Pleased to see you again, Maigret . . . I didn't know you were back in the job. A curious business, eh! She's waiting for you. She refuses to talk before she's seen you. It was she who telephoned the gendarmerie at around one o'clock this morning to announce that she had just killed her son-in-law.

'You'll see. She's as calm as if she had just made jam or cleaned out her cupboards.

'Actually she spent the night tidying up her things and, when I got here, her suitcase was packed.'

'Where are the others?'

'Her second son-in-law, Charles, is in the drawing room with his wife. The deputy public prosecutor and the examining magistrate are questioning them. They claim they know nothing, that the old lady had been acting strangely for a while.'

Maigret lumbered up the stairs and, something he rarely

did, he emptied his pipe and put it in his pocket before knocking at the door, where a second gendarme stood guard. It was a simple gesture, but it was a sort of homage to Bernadette Amorelle.

'What is it?'

'Detective Chief Inspector Maigret.'

'Let him come in.'

She had been left alone with her maid and, when Maigret went in, she was sitting at a pretty little writing desk, busy penning a letter.

'It's for my lawyer,' she said, apologizing. 'Leave us, Mathilde.'

The sun was streaming in through the three windows of this bedroom where the old woman had spent so many years. There was a joyful glint in her eyes and even – goodness knows if the moment might seem incongruous – a sort of playfulness.

She was pleased with herself. She was proud of what she had done. She had a slightly mocking attitude towards the burly inspector who, unlike her, would not have been capable of finishing things off.

'There was no other solution, was there?' she said. 'Sit down. You know that I hate talking to someone who is standing.'

Then, rising herself, blinking a little because of the dazzling sun in her eyes:

'Last night, when I finally got Aimée to tell me everything . . .'

He made the mistake of registering surprise. A flicker. A start at the mention of Aimée, Charles Malik's wife.

Madame Amorelle was as clever as Maigret and under-stood.

'I should have realized that you didn't know that. Where is Georges-Henry?'

'At my place, with my wife.'

'At your house in Meung?'

And she smiled at the memory of Maigret, whom she had mistaken for the gardener when she had gone to fetch him, having entered through the little green garden door.

'In Paris, in my apartment in Place des Vosges.'

'Does he know?'

'I told him before coming here.'

'What did he say?'

'Nothing. He's calm.'

'Poor boy! I wonder how he found the courage not to say anything. Don't you think it's funny, going to prison at my age? These gentlemen, by the way, are very kind. At first, they wouldn't believe me. They thought I was confessing to protect the real culprit. They nearly de-manded proof.

'It went very well. I don't know exactly what time it was. I had my pistol in my bag. I went over there. There was a light on the first floor. I rang the bell. Malik asked me what I wanted from the window.

'"To talk to you," I answered.

'I'm convinced he was frightened. He asked me to come back the next day, claiming that he wasn't feeling well, that he was suffering from neuralgia.

'"If you don't come down right away," I shouted, "I'll have you arrested."

'In the end he came down, in his pyjamas and dressing gown. Have you seen him?'

'Not yet.'

'I insisted: "Let's go into your study. Where is your wife?"

'"She's in bed. I think she's asleep."

'"Good."

'"Mother, are you sure this can't wait until tomorrow?"

'And do you know what I replied?

'"That won't do you any good. A few hours more, or less . . ."'

'He tried to follow. He was as cold as a pike. I've always said he was like a pike, but people laughed at me.

'He opened the door to his study.

'"Sit down," he said to me.

'"There's no need."

'Had he guessed what I was about to do? I'm convinced he had, because he automatically glanced at the desk drawer where he usually keeps his gun. If I'd given him the time, I'll wager that he would have defended himself and he would probably have shot first.

'"Listen, Malik," I went on. "I know about all your vile deeds. Roger is dead (Roger was Campois' son), your daughter is dead, your son . . ."'

Maigret had opened his eyes wide at the words *your daughter*. He had finally understood and he looked at the old woman with a stupefaction that he no longer sought to hide.

'"Since there's no other way out and no one had the guts to do it, it may as well be an elderly grandmother who takes care of it. Goodbye, Malik."

'And as I said the last word, I fired. He was three paces away from me. He clutched his stomach, because I shot too low. I squeezed the trigger two more times.

'He fell, and Laurence came rushing in, half-crazy.

'"There," I said to her. "Now we can live in peace and we can all breathe at last."

'Poor Laurence. I think it was a relief for her too. Aimée's the only one to shed any tears for him.

'"Call a doctor if you like, but I don't think there's any point," I continued. "He's well and truly dead! And if he weren't, I'd finish him off with a bullet through the brain. Now, I suggest you come and spend the rest of the night at our house. There's no need to call the servants."

'We both left. Aimée came running to meet us, while Charles stood in the doorway looking shifty.

'"What have you done, Mother? Why is Laurence . . . ?"

'I told Aimée. She suspected as much, after the conversation we had just had in my room. Charles didn't dare open his mouth. He followed us like a big dog.

'I came back here and telephoned the gendarmerie. They were very courteous.'

'So,' murmured Maigret after a silence, 'it's Aimée.'

'I'm just an old fool, I should have guessed. I'd always had my suspicions about Roger Campois, for example. At least that it was Malik who had got him into the habit of gambling.

'I was so thrilled, at the time, that he would be our son-in-law! He was more brilliant than the others. He was able to entertain me. My husband had the tastes of a petty bourgeois, a country bumpkin even, it was Malik who taught us how to live in style, who took us to Deauville. Before that, I had never set foot in a casino and I remember he gave me the first chips to play roulette.'

'He married Laurence—'

'Because Aimée was too young, wasn't she? Because she was only fifteen at the time? If Aimée had been two years older, Roger Campois might perhaps have lived. He would have married the older daughter and Malik the younger.'

They could hear people coming and going down below. Through the windows they saw a group heading for the Maliks' house, where the body still lay.

'Aimée truly loved him,' sighed Madame Amorelle. 'She still loves him, in spite of everything. She hates me now, for what I did last night.'

The skeleton in the cupboard! If there had only been, in that metaphorical cupboard, just the skeleton of the shy Roger Campois!

'When did he think of bringing his brother from Lyon to marry your youngest daughter?'

'Perhaps two years after his own marriage. And I was naive! I could see that Aimée was only interested in her brother-in-law, that she was much more in love with him than her sister was. Strangers mistook her for his wife, and when we travelled together, she was the one, despite her young age, that they called madame.

'Laurence wasn't jealous. She was blind to it, was happy to live in the shadow of her husband, whose personality crushed her.'

'So Monita was the daughter of Ernest Malik?'

'I found out yesterday. But there are other things that, at my age, I'd rather not know.'

This brother who was brought from Lyon, where he was just a low-wage earner and then married off to a rich heiress.

Did he know, at the time?

Probably! He's spineless, meek! He got married because he was told to get married. He acted as a screen! In exchange for playing the part of husband, he shared the Maliks' fortune with his brother.

So Ernest had two wives, and children in both homes.

And that was what Monita had found out. That was what had overwhelmed her with disgust and driven her to drown herself.

'I don't know exactly how she discovered the truth, but, since last night, I have an idea. Last week, I had the lawyer come to change my will.'

'Maître Ballu, I know—'

'I had not been getting along with the Maliks for a long time, and funnily enough it was Charles I hated the most. Why, I don't know . . . I'd always found him underhand. I was close to thinking that he was worse than his brother.

'I wanted to disinherit the pair of them, and leave my entire fortune to Monita.

'That same evening, Aimée admitted yesterday during the scene we had, Ernest came to see Charles to discuss the matter.

'They were very worried about this new will, whose contents they didn't know. They spent a long time talking in Charles' study on the ground floor. Aimée went up to bed. It was only much later, when her husband came up to bed that she said:

'"Hasn't Monita come back?"

'"Why do you say that?"

'"She didn't come up and say good night to me as usual."

'Charles went into the girl's room. She wasn't there and the bed hadn't been slept in. He went downstairs and found her in the lounge, ashen-faced, sitting in the dark as if frozen.

'"What are you doing here?"

'She appeared not to hear. She consented to go upstairs.

'I am convinced, now, that she had overheard everything. She knew. And the next morning, before anyone was up, she went out as if going for her swim, which she often did.

'Except that she didn't intend to swim.'

'And she'd had the opportunity to speak to her cousin . . . her cousin whom she loved and who is, in fact, her brother.'

There was a timid knock at the door. Bernadette Amorelle opened it and found herself facing the chief inspector from Melun.

'The car is downstairs,' he announced, not without some embarrassment, for it was the first time in his career that he had had to arrest an eighty-two-year-old woman.

'In five minutes,' she answered, as if she were speaking to her butler. 'We still have a few things to say to each other, my friend Maigret and I.'

When she went back to Maigret, she commented, demonstrating her astonishing alertness:

'Why haven't you smoked your pipe? You know very well that you can. I came to fetch you. I didn't know what was afoot. At first I wondered whether Monita had been killed because I had just made her my heiress. I confess to you – but this is none of their business, there are things that are none of their business – that I thought that they might want to poison me. There, inspector. There's still the boy. I'm pleased that you took care of him, for I can't get the idea out of my head that he would have ended up like Monita.

'Put yourself in their shoes . . . At their age, suddenly finding out . . .

'In the boy's case, it was even more serious. He wanted to know. Boys are more enterprising than girls. He knew that his father kept his private papers in a little cupboard in his bedroom and that he always kept the key on him.

'He forced the cupboard open, the day after Monita's death. It was Aimée who told me. Ernest Malik told her everything, he knew he could trust her, that she was worse than a slave.

'Malik realized the cupboard had been broken into and he immediately suspected his son.'

'What documents could he have found?' sighed Maigret.

'I burned them last night. I asked Laurence to go and fetch them, but Laurence didn't dare go back into the house where her husband's body lay.

'Aimée went.

'There were letters from her, little notes they passed to each other, arranging to meet.

'There were receipts signed by Roger Campois. Not

only did Malik lend him money to sink him further, but he got him loans from money-lenders, which he then redeemed.

'He kept all that.'

And, with contempt:

'Despite everything, he had the soul of a book-keeper!'

She did not understand why Maigret corrected her as he heaved himself to his feet:

'Of a tax collector!'

It was he who saw her into the car, and she extended her arm through the window to shake his hand.

'You're not too annoyed with me?' she asked as the police car pulled away, taking her to her prison.

And he never knew if she meant for having dragged him away from the peace and quiet of his garden in Meung-sur-Loire for a few days or for firing the gun.

There had been a skeleton in the cupboard for many years, and it was the old lady who had taken it upon herself to clean things up, like those grandmothers who can't bear the house to be dirty.

OTHER TITLES IN THE SERIES

CÉCILE IS DEAD
GEORGES SIMENON

'Barely twenty-eight years old. But it would be difficult to look more like an old maid, to move less gracefully, no matter how hard she tried to be pleasing. Those black dresses . . . that ridiculous green hat!'

For six months the dowdy Cécile has been coming to the police station, desperate to convince them that someone has been breaking into her aunt's apartment. No one takes her seriously – until Maigret unearths a story of merciless, deep-rooted greed.

Translated by Anthea Bell

OTHER TITLES IN THE SERIES

And more to follow